Brigham's Day

Brigham's Day

John Gates

Walker & Company *New York*

All the characters and events portrayed in this work are fictitious.
First published in the United States of America in 2000 by Walker Publishing Company, Inc.
Published simultaneously in Canada by Fitzhenry and Whiteside
Markham, Ontario L3R 4T8
Library of Congress Cataloging-in-Publication Data

Gates, John.
Brigham's day / John Gates
p. cm.
ISBN 0-8027-3344-1 (HC)
1. Mormon women—Fiction. 2. Mormons—Fiction. 3. Utah—Fiction.
I. Title.
PS3557.A875 B75 2000
813'.54—dc21 00-022876
CIP

Series design by M. J. DiMassi

Printed in the United States of America
2 4 6 8 10 9 7 5 3 1

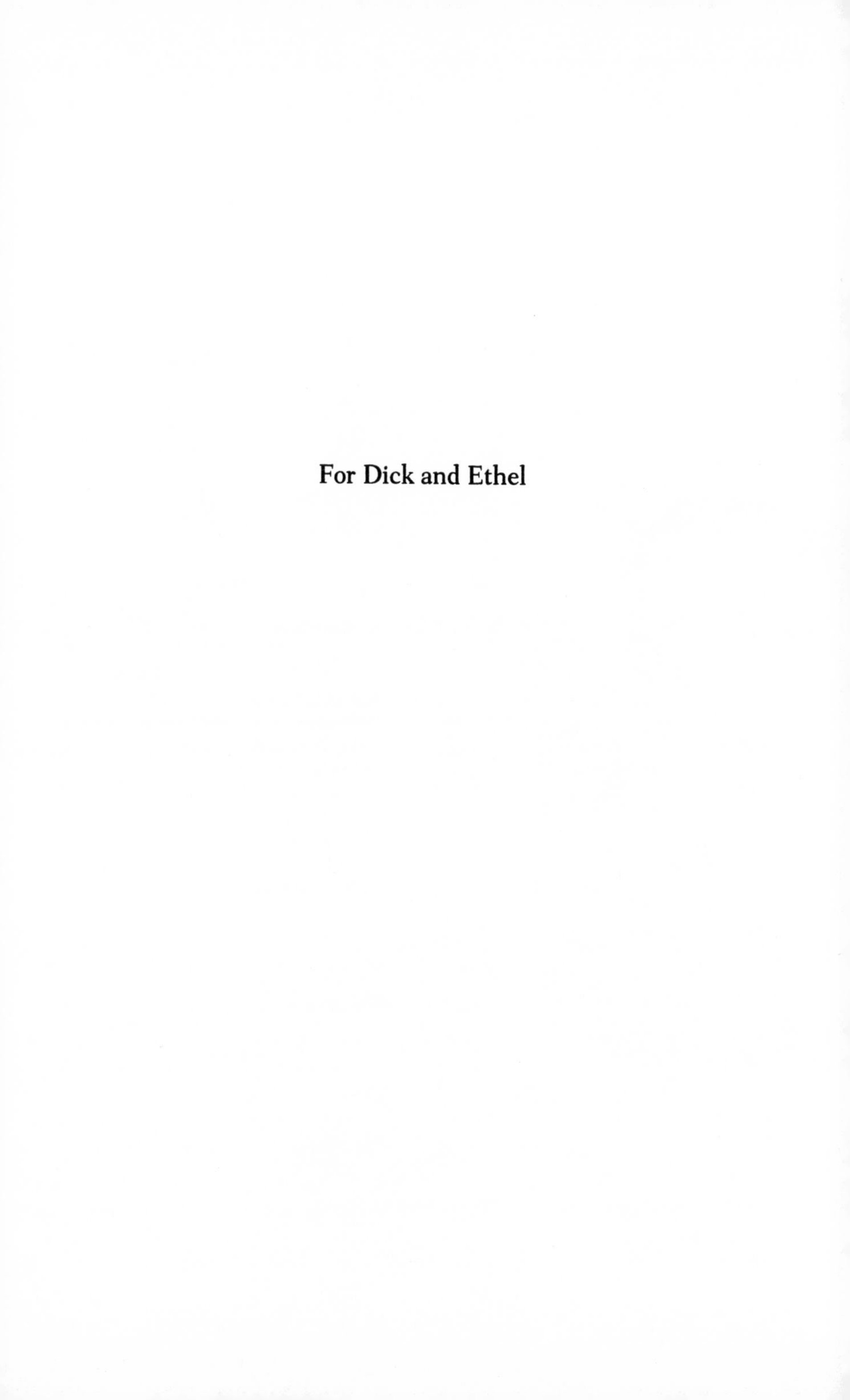

For Dick and Ethel

It is new moon and twilight,
I see the hiding of douceurs . . . I see nimble ghosts whichever way I look.

WALT WHITMAN

Acknowledgments

I am indebted to the scholarship of Juanita Brooks, in her book *The Mountain Meadows Massacre*; William Wise, in *Massacre at Mountain Meadows*; and Charles Kelly, editor of *Journals of John D. Lee*.

I also want to thank Cynthia Adams, Gabe Dellapiana, Bobby Perel, Mike Spurlock, Richard Von Hake, and Nancy Wodell for their encouragement and advice, and especially Ralph Dellapiana of the Salt Lake Public Defenders for allowing me to tap his considerable knowledge of Utah criminal law and procedure.

But above all, I owe the most to my agent, Philip Spitzer, who never lost faith, and to my wife, Ana, who inspires it.

Although Kanab, Utah, does certainly exist, as do other towns and some local business establishments mentioned, the present-day story is fictitious, the characters wholly imaginary.

But the horrifying events that occurred at Mountain Meadows in 1857 and 1877 are real, and with the exception of Josiah Lamb, so, too, are those souls who were there.

Brigham's Day

Prologue

MOUNTAIN MEADOWS, UTAH
MARCH 23, 1877, 10:16 A.M.

The meadow has changed in twenty years. The hills around it, once filled with queer shadows and impulse, have been scraped smooth by the floods of 1861 and 1873, and the livestock have stripped away the long grass that once danced in the wind like ribbons of silk. And the human bones and the knots of hair and the scraps of faded clothing, they too are gone, of course.

Now the March air sits cold and heavy, the half-frozen mud near the seeps cracks when the boots crush it, and a man sitting on the edge of the box shivers in a heavy coat, a hat, and a woolen muffler. The men near him huddle against the side of a wagon, waiting for the photographer to adjust his camera, while one of them prays softly to himself.

—Be still.

The shutter releases with a sharp, metallic sound as though something has broken, and the photographer steps away and thrusts his hands into his greatcoat.

—I have it.

The men watch the photographer remove his equipment, and one of them then frees himself from the group and walks over to the man sitting on the box.

—Well, John, that is over.

—It is. Have that man deliver a photograph each to my wives,

if he can do such a thing.

—I shall.

—Thank you, brother.

—Would you like to say a word, John?

—I would.

John rises slowly from the box and stands on the hard ground and loosens the muffler, despite the raw cold, and looks out at the low hills smeared with mud and streaked with trails the animals have made.

—I have but little to say this morning. My conscience is clear before God and man.

He pauses and watches the man named George return to the others near the wagon, where they all stamp their boots to keep their feet warm and wrap their coats tighter about them.

—I declare that I did everything in my power to save those people, but evidence has been brought against me which is as false as the hinges of hell. I have been sacrificed in a cowardly manner—

His voice catches, and he swallows and stares at the ground a few yards away, where the rocks from the soldiers' old makeshift monument lie strewn, some half buried in the mud. It had been ordered destroyed by Brother Brigham.

—I would have given worlds. . . .

Again he stops and shakes his head, still staring at the rocks.

—That is all.

At that, a man in a long, gray coat appears from behind one of the wagons and signals with his hand to another cluster of men, five of them, who have been standing in the open near a soldier in uniform. He walks up to John and places his hand on his shoulder. He is a large man, with a thick, black beard, and his breath explodes in vapor around his face.

—It is time, John.

—Yes, it is.

—I have been asked to inquire of you, for the last time, of . . . that which is sought.

John shakes his head. —I do not know of it. What was in the possession of Brother Lamb that awful day, only God knows. He street—the Pow-Wow, Trail's End, the Book Outpost, Duke's—and all had painted signs that jutted out over the sidewalk, perpendicular to the storefront. On his left, the church sat squarely in the middle of a grassy park, a centerpiece of sorts, a red-brick affair that also had a sign, one made of metal letters hammered into its front wall.

THE CHURCH OF JESUS CHRIST OF LATTER-DAY SAINTS

The instructions he had been given told him to turn left after the church, and he did so, and he saw the county courthouse immediately. It was an old two-story building, constructed of red brick on a red sandstone base, its windows tall and arched. In front, along a low wall made of the same sandstone blocks, was a graveled space, and he guided his Toyota there and turned off the engine. He was too tall for the car, and when he got out, he unfolded himself like a hinged contraption and stretched in the sunlight, turning his face to the sky, his eyes half closed.

He smoothed his white shirt, tucking it into his slacks, then walked to the front of the building and opened the heavy door. Despite the brilliance of the day outside, the interior of the courthouse was dark, the smell of old paper and furniture oil making it seem even darker. The wooden floors creaked as he moved across them, and finding no one on duty in any of the offices, he walked up a set of stairs to the second floor. At the end of a dim hallway he saw an open door, and he walked there and looked in.

A man sat behind a desk, the light from the tall window behind him so bright that it almost made him look like a silhouette, a shadow-creature.

"Reed."

The man at the desk turned his head, and as he did, the reflected light struck his face, glinting off his glasses. He looked to be about sixty years old, thin, with silvery hair, and he smiled and stood up. He wore a white shirt and narrow tie.

"Brig," he said. "Cripes, I didn't think you'd get here so soon." He stuck a pale hand out across the desk, letting it hover

over the nameplate that read HON. REED MACKLEPRANG.

"Come in."

The man at the door stepped into the room, and as he extended his hand, he saw another man sitting in a chair in the half-darkness. He was partially bald, with thick lips and tiny, bulging eyes, and he was dressed in a beige suit.

The judge shook hands and then pointed at the man sitting down. "This is the prosecutor on the case, DeWitt Hightower." He moved his finger again. "This is Brig Bybee, the new defense counsel we were talking about."

Hightower remained seated. He looked mean and humorless, his flesh a bright pink, as though scalded from something boiling inside.

"I've heard about you," Hightower said. He leaned forward and shook Bybee's hand.

"DeWitt's a good man," Mackleprang said. "He's out of Salt Lake."

Bybee studied the man's fishlike face. "City. Not the lake."

"Yeah," Hightower said.

"DeWitt was in Vietnam, too," the judge said to Bybee. He was beaming, like a parent bragging about two siblings, and he turned to Hightower. "Brig got himself some medals over to thar."

Bybee waited a beat, hoping that Hightower would not begin the ritualistic sniffing, the probing of the past—years, units, familiar battles—but the prosecutor only stood and picked up a battered leather briefcase from the floor.

"Well, good for you," Hightower said. He walked to the door, but stopped and looked at Mackleprang, his bleak eyes bulging. "It smells like spit in here, Reed. You can smell spit."

"I don't spit," Mackleprang said. He swept a hand around the office, one used only once or twice a year for the occasional trial in Kane County. "Besides, this isn't mine. I'm just here on loan, like you. You know that."

Without responding, Hightower turned and left, and the other two men listened to him descend the stairs, his footsteps echoing through the old building.

Mackleprang turned back to Bybee. "DeWitt's a good man."

"Seems like it."

"Anyway, thanks for coming so soon."

"It was a court order," Bybee said.

Mackleprang sat down, making his chair squeak in the quiet room, and inspected the other man, like a prospective buyer looking for obvious damage. Bybee was tall and slender, but rugged looking, with straight, squared shoulders, long arms, and strong, sun-darkened hands. And although he had a barely noticeable paunch, he displayed a full head of black hair, just a smear of gray at the temples, and only his wire-rimmed bifocals hinted at his true age.

"You look well, Brig," Mackleprang said. "Fit. Sit." He laughed at his rhyme and pointed at a chair.

Bybee sat down and pushed back a clump of black hair that had fallen across his forehead. "I don't feel fit."

"Wol . . . I'm sorry," Mackleprang said. "How's life up in Beaver? Staying busy?"

Bybee did not answer at once. The judge knew he was not busy; he knew that, after the Sipes debacle, he was scrambling just to pay his overhead, accepting court appointments and *ad litem* work, even doing his own typing or word processing, or whatever they called it these days, to save on a secretary's salary.

"Real busy," Bybee finally said.

The judge pursed his lips as though he had just bitten into something sour, spoiled. "That's good," he said, and his head began bobbing, as though it were attached to a spring and someone had given it a gentle tap. "Good . . . good."

Neither spoke for several moments, and in the silence, Bybee leaned back in the old government-gray chair, its armrests worn black, and studied the man across from him, a man he had known for twenty years, a traveling judge, like a circuit rider. At that short distance—the width of the desk—Mackleprang looked sleek and clever, an elder who belonged in power, in the church's Quorum of the Twelve, maybe, some groomed statesman. But if you bent closer and examined the face behind the pink-tinted glasses, he seemed dull, lost, his eyes distant, as though he were concentrating on something, maybe a voice in his head.

"I heard about you and Helena," Mackleprang said. He contorted his face into a caricature of concern. "Cripes, a shame. A real shame. You-all had been married a long time, I guess."

"Twenty-seven years," Bybee said. Helena might calculate it differently, he knew, considering that she viewed the marriage as legitimate and viable only when Bybee was involved with the church, truly involved, not just appearing at ward hall picnics or taking Boy Scouts up to Duck Creek.

Through the window behind the judge, Bybee saw an orange crane slowly swing into view and stop, a chain and wrecking ball dangling, and he pointed at it, signaling a change in topic. "What's going on?"

The judge looked over his shoulder and then swiveled back around, his old chair squealing. "County's getting ready to tar this courthouse down. In fact, as soon as this trial's over. It'll be the last case ever tried in this old dump."

"Why don't you just dismiss the case now and let them get started?"

Mackleprang shook his head, frowning. "Can't do that."

"I was kidding."

The judge said nothing, and Bybee listened to the silence of the old place, feeling its decay, as he often felt his own. All it needed was an old, rasping clock in the hallway that loudly ticked away, counting down the final moments.

"Let's talk about this case," Bybee said, and he pushed his glasses up along his thin, straight nose.

"Okay," Mackleprang said, and almost as a counterpoint, removed his own glasses and then put them on again. "The defendant's lawyer—one of them, Furl Shields—just withdrew. Personality problems—"

"Furl? His name was . . . *Furl*?"

"Yeah." Mackleprang hesitated, confused. "Anyway, there were personality problems with his cocounsel. Mormon, non-Mormon thing."

"Surprise."

"Things were getting pretty tense, I hear. This is the first murder—ever—in this county. A bad murder."

"As opposed to a good murder."

The judge twisted his pale hands together on the desk and looked at the lawyer's tanned, handsome face, the same face—almost the same pose—that he had seen almost every day in the newspapers during the Sipes trial two years ago: the dark eyes narrowed, the mouth slightly open to show straight, white teeth, and the head cocked, as though listening, sensing the statewide religious wrath that was about to rumble down upon him like an avalanche.

"Look, your guy's name is Owen Parks," Mackleprang said. "He was—is—a drifter, a kid, bumming around down har, working for a few of the ranchers—odd-job stuff, mowing alfalfa, some baling, was even riding up on these ranges to run some cattle and—"

Bybee only half listened, soothed by the judge's accent—what some called a Mormon accent—a soft, near-lisping talk mixed in with a western drawl, one that seemed to lull the listener, luring him.

"—worked for an old man named Douglas Farnsworth now and then, over to a place called Hell's Bellows." The judge jerked his thumb over his shoulder. "About ten miles east of town."

Bybee nodded knowledgeably; he had never been in this part of the state before, despite the fact that Beaver and Kanab were fierce high school football rivals, each community descending upon the other every other year.

"Farnsworth had been the local bishop once, a stubborn old guy, everyone says. Kind of crazy. Yelled across the street at people he saw smoking. Stuff like that."

"Sounds like my father."

"Wol, Parks was always going on about the old man, raising a stink over to a place called the Red Land Roost, whar he stayed, kind of a big lot outside of town with trailers and campers . . . all of that. He was threatening him, yelling. Anyway, last Thanksgiving—" He paused. "*Thanksgiving Day*, Brig, a man named Wester Lewis, another old man over to

Hell's Bellows, he went to visit Farnsworth in the evening and found him dead in his basement, shot through the head."

"And?"

"And some Navs over to this Red Land Roost will testify that Parks had a pistol and about the threats. And then thar's this."

Mackleprang opened a desk drawer, withdrew a dirty envelope, and handed it to Bybee. It had the words "Parks, O," scribbled in one corner, and in the other, several numbers and letters.

"DeWitt wanted you to see it," Mackleprang said.

"DeWitt's a good man."

Bybee lifted the flap and pulled out a single photograph, a Polaroid, showing an old man in jeans and a work shirt lying on his side, a heaping of cans and wires around him. One eye was visible, open, and through the wispy layers of his white hair, a trickle of blood ran from a tiny, dark hole in the side of his head and down into patches of white beard that stuck to his jaw like lint.

Bybee flipped the photograph over; it was blank, and he laid it on the judge's desk. "This all the cops took?"

"Brig," Mackleprang said. "The sheriff didn't take this pitcher. It was found in Parks's camper."

Bybee made a face, knitting his thick eyebrows together, and picked up the photograph again and studied it. The body of the old man lay in a strange light—obviously from a flashbulb—and the dark edges of the picture showed a saddle, maybe, and the leg of a table.

"You're saying that Parks took this picture?"

"Yes."

"And carried it back to his trailer and—"

"His camper—"

"—left it where anyone could find it."

"Looks that way."

Bybee laughed, suddenly, remembering a misdemeanor case he had tried years before in Beaver, where his client, after stealing a new tire from a service station, had rolled it home across a vacant lot. The police had simply followed the tracks to the clod's house.

"Well," Bybee said, "why didn't Parks just leave his business card on the body?"

The judge shook his head. "Parks didn't have business cards."

"I was kidding, Reed." Bybee hesitated, wondering for a moment why the prosecutor would entrust the safekeeping of such critical evidence to the judge rather than his own files. "The search good?"

The judge nodded. "Yep. Even a warrant. Looks like a slam dunk."

"Oh, yeah?" Bybee said. He widened his dark eyes and cocked his head. "Did the cops find the camera?"

"No."

"The gun?"

"No. But, like I said, the Navs—"

"They test his hands for powder?"

"I don't know."

"Fingerprints?"

"No."

Bybee took the Polaroid and pressed his index finger into the corner of it, and held it up to the light, angling it. "Look, there's a print right there."

"Wol—"

"Anything of Parks's in that basement?"

"I don't think so. Place was torn apart, though. Top to bottom."

"Confession?"

"No."

"Well, that's not a slam dunk, then," Bybee said. "Maybe a short jump shot."

Mackleprang seemed unsettled, and he put his hands palm down on the desk, as though he were keeping it from rising. "A man died, Brig."

Bybee began to argue with this layman-like analysis of guilt, but he knew that, with most juries, the simplicity of sudden, violent death was evidence enough. "Well, anyway, for the record," Bybee said, "he didn't *die*. He was murdered. What else?"

The judge squinted at a calendar on the wall, one with a photograph of a red-haired girl in pigtails holding two kittens under the name AIKEN IMPLEMENT, and beneath that, the word *July*. "That's about it. As I said in my letter, the trial starts the twenty-first—" He looked at the calendar. "Twelve days from now." He made a wobbly grin. "That should be enough time for an old pro like you."

Bybee knew he could formally fight his appointment to the case by seeking relief from another court—a restraining order, maybe, or a writ of some kind. But he needed the money, as little as it was going to be.

" 'Old' is right," he said. "Too old for this. I'm fifty-two." He waited for the postured surprise he usually received at the revelation of his age, the disclaimer, that head-shaking disbelief that he—rangy and athletic-looking—was firmly mired in middle age. But it never came, and the judge only blinked stupidly at him.

"So," Bybee said. "What's the name of my second chair?"

Mackleprang made the odd movement with his lips again, as though he were going to spit. "Ronnie Watters. But he's not—"

"I've heard of him," Bybee said, nodding. "A wild man."

"Wol, yeah." Mackleprang's hands were suddenly knotted together, his face troubled. "Look, Brig, Watters isn't second char. He's first. He's lead counsel."

For a moment, Bybee thought the blunted Mackleprang was, for once, exercising a sense of humor, but the judge's face was pinched with sympathy, or worry. At the same time, Bybee felt the heat start in his scalp and drain through him, down his face and neck and chest until it settled in his gut and churned there. Then the room actually seemed to shift, as though jarred by the wrecking ball hanging outside.

"You're assigning me as copilot?"

"Yeah. I'm sorry, Brig. I'd like you as lead, but you're still on probation with the state bar. They told me you can't be assigned as lead. I'm sorry. I wish you could be."

Bybee closed his eyes for a moment, absorbing yet another emotional grenade, one of dozens that had been lobbed at him since the Sipes trial. "Reed, I've been first-chairing murder cases for twenty years."

"I know, Brig. It's just . . . the rules. The law, I guess. They've got a string on your license."

"But Watters is a kid, a baby lawyer. He's some crazy man out of control."

"I know. I know. That's one reason I want you on the case. Settle him down. Keep him straight. Use your experience. Besides, he's been working on this for several months."

Bybee could feel his eyes burn, and he closed them for a moment. He opened them, half expecting the judge to be gone, this bad dream over.

"Look," Mackleprang said. He held his hands out for a moment, like a prophet, a good ward bishop administering to his flock. "I'm giving you a chance to . . . I don't know . . . *prove* yourself again. Rebuild. Forget all that junk in the past. Sink your teeth into something. It'll just take a case or two. I'm serious."

"So am I," Bybee said. He felt leaden, weighed down by a dragging humiliation, a long cloak that seemed, each time he turned, to take on heavier, more mortifying dimensions. "I can't do this."

"Brig, you came within a har of getting booted out of the business a few months ago. Did you know that? Whether you like it or not, you're hanging by a thread with the bar. You're going to have to do this."

Bybee didn't answer. He concentrated instead on the judge's repeated imagery—strings, threads, hairs—as though, rather than grounded by the dragging cloak, he swung recklessly through life from one fragile filament to the next, each ready to snap at any moment.

"Just get into it," the judge said. "Just grab on to something for—"

Bybee lifted his head, suddenly, and the same stubborn tuft of black hair fell across his face. "For what, Reed? For a *change*? For *once*?"

"Wol, you're just going to have to do this," Mackleprang said again.

Bybee took a slow breath to calm himself. He knew the judge was right; he really had no choice, and as he sat back in the chair, smoothing his hair in place, he heard a squealing from outside, something shrill and fluttering, like a giant bird wheeling just over the courthouse, cawing. He looked out the window and saw the crane moving, its gears and parts grinding together, and then he saw the hand-lettered sign on the crane's metal ribs: KAIBAB SALVAGE, INC.

"You in the salvage business, Reed? Soul salvage?"

Mackleprang smiled. "Aren't we all? Hey, it won't be that bad. Watters is a little nutty, but . . ." He trailed off and leaned across the desk, lowering his voice like a conspirator. "Look, I don't want to try this case again because of some screwup. You know, Watters pulling some weird, bonehead play that gets me reversed." He drew himself up and tried to look serious, judicial. "I want Parks to get a far trial—the state, too—but I want a *standard* trial, by the book, no . . . crazy stuff. You're levelheaded, laid-back, maybe too laid-back—always have been—but you're a pro, and I need a pro. Watters needs a pro."

Bybee closed his eyes again, shielding himself from Mackleprang's clumsy patronizing, and envisioned himself waiting for Watters on the courthouse steps each day, to greet him, to straighten his tie, and later, to whisper courtroom instructions in his ear: "*Object. Object!*"

"Lord, Reed."

"Watters wants to meet you—today. He wanted to go to a place just outside of town, across the state line, a bar, but I said you war—" He stopped, unsure of the etiquette, the proper, polite term.

"Sober," Bybee said. "It's not a bad word. I have been for a year now."

Mackleprang's head began bobbing again. "Good, good, that's good. Anyway, he said he would be over to a place called the Trail's End instead, a café, at three o'clock." He pointed to his left. "Just down the street."

"Three o'clock," Bybee repeated. He stood up, his long legs weak now, the upper half of his body seemingly twice its weight, out of balance. "You said in your letter that you would reserve me a motel room."

The judge also rose. "I did."

Bybee waited. "And?"

"Brig, this place is jammed up with tourists. Japs and Germans everywhar. Cripes, I barely got me a room this morning."

Bybee squinted at him and cocked his head. He had represented defendants in little backwaters like this before, and the judges in those cases usually drove in the night before the trial—if not that very day.

"Why are you here so damn early, Reed?"

Mackleprang shrugged. "Little vacation, I guess. Country's real pretty around har, doing some sightseeing." He shook his head. "Anyway, the only place I could find for you is called the Piute Villa."

Bybee leaned toward the other man as though he were ducking. "The place I saw coming in? The tepees?"

"Wol, yeah. I tried to get you in at this Parry—"

"A tepee?" Bybee drooped, the humiliation complete. "Why don't I just sleep out in the park?"

"You can't. City won't allow it."

"I was kidding."

Bybee turned and walked out to the darkened hallway and stopped next to an oaken pew. The judge followed halfway and stood in the doorway, the shadow from the open transom falling across part of his face.

"Brig, I need to tell you that's thar's lots of rumors flying around about this case."

"Like what?"

"Like . . . crazy stuff. Weird stuff. Don't listen to them. I don't want you sidetracked. Just let things run thar course. A standard trial. You know."

"Well, I'm not sure I *do* know," Bybee said.

"Wol, anyway, I appreciate it," Mackleprang said. He pointed down the darkened hallway. "The court clerk, Thurma, I think that's her name, has some paperwork for you to fill out, if you can ever find her. Tax stuff. You also should drop by and see the sheriff. Introduce yourself. His name is Lamar Little; he and his deputy—his son, LeGrand—worked the case up. LeGrand'll probably be the new sheriff, come November."

Bybee turned around and began walking down the hall, and then stopped and faced Mackleprang. "Furl, LeGrand, Thurma," he said. "Is there a contest on or something? Goofiest Mormon name?"

"C'mon. You should know better."

"So long, Reed."

Mackleprang shifted so that he was now perfectly framed by the door, still backlit from his window, a shadow-creature again.

"So long . . . *Brigham.*"

Bybee thumped down to the first floor and out into the brilliant sunlight, shading his eyes with his hand, walked to his car, and stopped. A mustard-yellow envelope—a ticket—had been wedged beneath one wiper blade, and a blue-and-white patrol car, the word SHERIFF painted on the side, sat parked beside him, the motor running. Inside, behind the wheel, sat a young, blond-haired man in a gray uniform, a pair of sunglasses hiding half of his face.

"No parking here," the officer said through the open window. He had a partially grown beard—thin and adolescent—and he smiled. "Obey the law, Mr. Bybee."

"How did you know my name?"

The officer did not answer and, instead, shifted the car into gear with a loud *thunk*. "City ordinance," he said.

He slowly backed away, and as he did, Bybee saw another man in the car, in the back. He was a bloated, fleshy thing in the same gray uniform, sprawled across the seat, half sitting. As the car straightened and moved down the street, the man turned and looked at Bybee through the rear window, his huge, bearded face twisted sideways at an odd angle, as though his neck were broken.

"It's not a city," Bybee said, to no one.

2

LONG before tourists discovered Kanab and the canyon country around it, Hollywood film companies trooped into town every spring and summer to shoot their westerns, and the movies became as much a part of the little town as alfalfa and cattle.

Then, when the westerns died out, the old-timers would sit at Peach's Café, now called the Trail's End, and brag about the movies they were in: *Drums along the Mohawk, The Lone Ranger, Westward the Women*, and dozens more. Sneaking cups of coffee, they joked of those strange summer days of famous actresses swimming nude in the bottomless lake outside town, of the boozing, the extravagance; and then they would hunch closer and whisper the dark tales of seduction, of outright rape, of the rumored liaison between a bosomy Kanab tart and a greasy leading man—probably Viola Cram and Victor Mature.

These jawboners in their John Deere ball caps still sit and talk of the days when the drowsy little Mormon town that Brigham Young and Buffalo Bill Cody had once visited was a microcosm of the seething world beyond the cliffs, a world of Sodom, of the Gentiles, of gluttony and glamour.

And a motel called Parry Lodge, just across the street, had been its frantic center point, only two blocks from the LDS church.

Bybee could not find a parking spot on the street, so he swung his Toyota into the Parry Lodge parking lot and drove past the rooms there. Each had a hand-painted sign above the door with the name of an actor who had once slept there, and he crept slowly through as though he were in a gallery: the Ray Milland Room, the Lloyd Nolan Room, Ava Gardner, Glenn Ford, Coburn, Stanwyck, Wayne. . . .

He finally found a white-lined space between the Randolph Scott Room and the Maureen O'Hara Room. He got out, not bothering to lock his doors, walked to the curb at Center Street, and waited until the traffic cleared; then, when there was a short break, he loped across the street to the Trail's End and opened the door.

The place was noisy and crowded, half of it filled with the jawboners and the other half with tourists, as Mackleprang had warned, mostly Europeans in dark shirts and sandals, and a group of Japanese in one corner. And, like every other café in this part of the world, the place was decorated in faux western: wagon wheel chandeliers, branding irons on the walls, and off to one side, a quarter-size Conestoga, the "Salad Wagon," filled with plastic tubs of limp vegetables and a canister of salad dressing that looked like a pail of semen.

A waitress approached him, a teenage girl in boots, blue jeans, and a cowboy hat. An old six-gun jutted out from a leather holster that sloped across her buttocks.

"War full up," she said. She did not look at him, but stared out the window as she ran her fingers across a row of pimples on her chin.

Bybee smiled at her. "Said Saint Peter."

The girl did not understand, and Bybee looked past her, spotting a man in a green shirt sitting alone in a booth in the rear. He was waving one hand, a toothy grin seeming to overtake his whole face, and pointing at himself with the other. Bybee nodded at the girl and walked around her, past a table where three men were arguing in French, and came up to the booth, the gun-toting waitress trailing him like a bodyguard, frowning.

"You Watters?" Bybee said.

The man in the green shirt was still grinning. He was big and blond, a tuft of chest hair sprouting up at his open collar, and would have been handsome, arguably, if not for the size of his teeth—big, uneven things that filled his mouth.

"Sure am," Watters said. Although the sleeves of his shirt were short, they sagged beyond his elbows, and both of his tanned forearms rested on a yellow legal pad. He suddenly thrust out his right hand—large and golden-haired—and, as Bybee expected, nearly crushed his own. "And you're Brig Bybee." His voice, predictably, was loud, and he showed more of his teeth. "Sit down, my friend."

Bybee slid into the opposite side of the booth, and Watters picked up a cup of coffee and continued to stare at him as he sipped at it. Bybee turned to the waitress with the six-gun. "I'll have coffee, too."

The waitress began to leave, but Watters reached out and grabbed her arm, stopping her. He pointed at the woman's gun and then moved his finger, aiming it at her crotch, where the pants were molded to her in a deep, denim cleft.

"That thing work, hon?" He glanced at Bybee.

"No," the waitress said, and she gently pulled her arm away.

"Huh. Thought it might. Hey, look, you serve beer here?"

"No. I told you that before."

"Too bad," Watters said. "You sure?"

"I'm shore."

He pointed at the woman's pistol again, and then openly stared at her shirt, at the glimpse of a white bra between the buttons. "Well, you've got the gun, hon."

The waitress exhaled theatrically and walked away, the wooden grip of her pistol rotating in tiny circles.

Watters turned back to Bybee. "Bitch."

Bybee looked away. "You wanted to meet?"

"Yeah, sure did, my friend. Thanks for coming over."

Watters drummed his thick fingers on the tabletop, appraising Bybee the same way Mackleprang had, looking for scars or wounds, and then leaned back in the booth.

"Mackleprang says you're from Beaver," Watters said. "Never met anyone from Beaver."

"Well, now you have," Bybee said. He tried to figure out the faint pattern on Watters's ugly shirt. "And you?"

"Ogden," Watters said. "You married? Kids?"

"Was. I've got a daughter. She just got married." Bybee paused again. "You?"

Watters violently shook his head, as if chasing away gnats. "Nope. No kids, either." His teeth seemed to slide out, downward, and then spread out. "Not that I know of."

Bybee did not laugh at this old line, and the two fell silent for a moment, both gazing over the other man's shoulder.

"Mackleprang says you got some kind of medals in Vietnam," Watters said.

Bybee laughed out loud. "Just air medals, nothing heroic. Fly fast and low, don't get too excited, keep the aircraft and crew in one piece—and you get one. Simple."

Watters nodded appreciatively and lifted his coffee cup. "I'd like to see one sometime."

"A helicopter?"

"No, the medal," Watters said, and he waited, expectantly, as though Bybee might rip open his shirt and show one right now, dangling against his chest on its tattered ribbon. But he didn't even have the medals anymore; they had become lost or discarded—like everything else, of late.

"Maybe someday," Bybee said.

"Okay." Watters still kept his eyes on Bybee's face, half narrowed, as though he suspected the man might be an impostor. Bybee leaned back in the seat and stared steadily at the other man, his thin face unmoving, his dark eyes locked in some silly contest with the eyes across the table.

Finally Watters fumbled inside his shirt pocket and brought out a crumpled pack of Marlboros and a book of matches. "You care if I smoke?"

Bybee looked at the rest of the room and shook his head. "I don't think you're supposed to here."

"You mean *here*, in the restaurant?" Watters said. He put the unlit cigarette in his mouth. "Or *here* in the town . . . or, *here*, on this earth?" The cigarette jumped as he talked, like a tiny baton emphasizing his words.

"In the restaurant."

"All right," Watters said. He dropped the cigarette and the pack and the matches back into his pocket. "Just testing."

"Okay."

Watters continued to appraise the man, cocking his head. "I followed the Bellard Sipes trial. You did a hell of a job."

"I lost, Watters."

"Call me Ronnie. Yeah, I know, but you busted the church's nuts, anyway." He leaned forward again and lowered his voice. "Tell me the God's truth. Was Sipes really banging that little girl?"

"Yes, he was."

Watters grinned, satisfied. "Like a cheap gong, I bet. God, he's an ugly son of a bitch."

Bybee found himself unconsciously nodding, agreeing. The newspapers had been filled with Sipes's picture back then: the thick body, the bald head, the dark suit and black, heavy-rimmed glasses that made one of the youngest members—ever—of the First Presidency, a man of God, look like a professional wrestler at a wedding, a mob hit man. Or just a plain, ugly son of a bitch, as Watters had just observed.

"Goddamned hypocrites get away with murder," Watters said. He laughed, suddenly. "Rape, too. You should've won."

"Jury didn't think so."

"Juries are fucked, my friend. You probably had an all-Mo jury. Mos aren't going to pop some big shot in the church. One of their own. Shit, no."

Bybee looked away, irritated. It seemed as if everyone in Utah—in the country—had some blurred rationale for the Sipes verdict, for the disaster. But Bybee—and the state bar—knew the real reason.

"So what about the *all-Mo* jury we're going to get in this case?" Bybee said. "How many minutes will it take them to convict this guy?"

"Maybe they won't. We have a lot to work with."

"Like what?"

"The state has no real evidence other than a Polaroid found in Parks's camper or trailer, or whatever the hell it is."

"I've seen it."

Watters frowned. "The camper?"

"No. The Polaroid. Mackleprang showed it to me."

"Okay. Well, that's just a little bit too obvious, don't you think?"

"Maybe not," Bybee said. "I've seen stupider things. Murderers aren't known for their intelligence."

"But no camera was found."

Watters, Bybee realized, like any defense attorney, had the same doubts and questions about the investigation and the state's case against Parks that he had. But his second-chair status rankled, burned at his gut, and plinking away at this buffoon like a jealous child helped salve that misery . . . somewhat.

"So?" Bybee said.

"So I imagine you can match a camera to a picture. Like a gun to a slug."

"What else?"

"No witnesses."

Bybee snorted, the way a law school professor would at a cocky student in a criminal evidence class. "Murders aren't committed on a stage. State doesn't need a witness, anyway. You know that."

"Parks has an alibi," Watters said. "He says he was with some Navs all afternoon. Local quack doctor says Farnsworth was killed around five."

"Alibis are usually a joke. Besides, Mackleprang says the Indians claim something different."

Watters winked. "I'm looking into that."

"Have you talked to them?"

"Who? The Navs? No, not yet. Like I say, I'm looking into it."

Bybee narrowed his eyes, finding it difficult to believe that Watters had not yet interviewed critical witnesses and had probably not even filed the requisite alibi notice. "What else are you looking into?" he said.

"I think Parks has been set up."

Bybee took a deep, exaggerated breath, as the waitress had done a moment before. He believed that if all convicted murderers were buried in a mass grave and had to agree on a representative epitaph on the common gravestone, it would have to be *I WAS SET UP*.

"Set up by whom?" Bybee said. "Jack Ruby?"

"Who?"

Watters looked truly confused, and Bybee realized that the lawyer had not even been born when Kennedy took office. "Nothing," Bybee said. "I'm kidding. So who's setting him up?"

At that moment, the waitress appeared with a cup of coffee and a handful of tiny tubs of creamer and plopped them on the table, shyly smiling at Bybee before she left. While Watters sat, waiting, restless, Bybee concentrated on opening the containers and dumping them, one by one, into the coffee, deliberately stalling, doing anything to irritate the man. When he finished, he looked up and straightened his glasses, and Watters leaned forward, lowering his voice.

"There's lots of talk around town. Some people believe that an old . . . I don't know . . . Mormon secret police, like a terrorist group, a posse, from the eighteen hundreds, is still around. They might have killed Farnsworth, blamed it—"

"Secret police?"

"Secret *fucking* police, man!" Watters said. He was sitting up, excited.

Bybee took a sip of his coffee and closed his eyes, not sure if he was really sitting in a cow-town café with a big, smirking jock, talking about secret police.

Bybee opened his eyes. "So what's this—"

"It's called the Daughter of Zion."

Bybee leaned back in the booth. He remembered the odd, feminine name from his childhood, from the Primary classes, where foursquare, humorless men in glasses and white shirts—men like Reed Mackleprang—taught all the squirming LDS kids the religion's sanitized theology: the First Vision, the Angel Moroni, the gold plates, the Urim and Thummim.

But then, after class, on the way home, the older boys whispered the church's real ghost stories: Haun's Mill, Joe Smith's lynching, the Mountain Meadows Massacre . . . the Daughter of Zion.

"It's a ghost story," Bybee said.

"Maybe not."

"I see. They ride out of the canyons at midnight, a full moon. They have no eyes, hooks for hands."

"You can laugh, my friend. This outfit might still be around."

"You really believe that?"

"Shit," Watters said. He held his hand out, palm upward, and swept it in a half circle. "Go poking around town. A lot of people believe that."

"A lot of people believe in flying saucers," Bybee said.

Watters winked again. "I know. I do."

Bybee picked up his coffee and licked the dry rim of the mug before drinking. Across the restaurant, their waitress was now standing at the Frenchmen's table, dodging their giggling attempts to touch her gun. She probably believed, Bybee guessed, that the rest of the world blurred and began to evaporate just beyond the red cliffs that seemed to encircle this town, and a Frenchman or a Japanese or a German was no more interesting than some hayseed farmer from up the valley at Panguitch or Circleville—or some LDS bogeymen resurrected from the past.

"So," Bybee said, setting his cup down, "why would some . . . Mormon Ku Klux Klan gun down a fellow Mormon out in the middle of nowhere?"

"Ah! There's the rub!" Watters said. He looked pleased, as though he had been waiting all afternoon to use the expression. He leaned forward again. "Because people say he had something that this Daughter of Zion wanted."

"Like what?" Bybee said. "An idea for a new name?"

"No, no."

"I was kidding, Watters."

"Oh, okay. Call me Ronnie. I don't know what Farnsworth was supposed to have. It's just the rumor. But there's this granddaughter—"

"Let me get this straight," Bybee said. "You want to go into trial and prove up a bunch of rumors?"

Watters shrugged. "Hell, if it'll work—yeah."

Bybee sadly shook his head and dropped his eyes to Watters's shirt. He studied it for a moment and then realized that the strange pattern was a hodgepodge of overlapping happy faces, faint and nearly invisible, as if the creatures were trapped inside, smiling through the cloth.

"You ever tried a murder case before?" Bybee said.

"Yeah, a couple." The insult apparently thudded off him. "Won one."

"Then you should know better. You can't waltz into a courtroom—especially here, in South Jesus—and start raving about . . . little green men."

"Sure you can, my friend," Watters said. "It's called comparative lunacy. I do it all the time."

"Comparative lunacy?"

"You bet. It means that you prove that everything around the crime is as weird and fucked up as the defendant. You prove that the world—in this case, Kanab, Utah—is a loony bin; that everyone in that courtroom, including the judge, is a liar or a lunatic. You convince the jury that the inmates have taken over the asylum and so every swingin' dick should be let out."

"That's crazy," Bybee said.

"It's supposed to be." Watters raised his hands above his head, revealing big, dark sweat stains under his armpits. "The whole world's gone mad! The sky is falling! Let's all get the hell out of here and go home!"

Bybee glanced around to see if anyone had been watching them. "That's crazy," he said again. He felt a true, rising antipathy for the rabbit-toothed loudmouth in front of him. "You just told me about all the problems with this case; I saw that as soon as Mackleprang briefed me. That's a foothold, something to work with. You can create some doubt in the jury's mind, maybe. But if you go in there and start spouting all this secret posse crap, you'll prove up this lunacy stuff, all right. They'll think *you're* crazy as hell."

Watters had been smiling through it all, and now his face suddenly changed, hardened, an instant transformation. "Right," he said. "No more crazy than some asshole filing a lawsuit against some guy that might be the next president of the Mormon church."

Bybee glared at Watters for a moment and then angrily pointed a finger at him. "That was different. I had evidence, facts—" He stopped, realizing how absurd—how pitiable—he sounded, trying to justify one of his rare forays into true commitment, one that exploded in his face.

"Right," Watters said again. "Tell that to those newspapers."

Bybee looked out across the café. During the Sipes trial, the pro-Mormon *Deseret News* had repeatedly printed a cartoon of Bybee mounted on a horse, in medieval armor, aiming a lance at the windmill-topped Salt Lake Temple. And then, after the verdict, the editors printed the same caricature, only this time he was slumped on his horse, the lance broken, and it had a simple caption under it: "Bye-bye, Bybee."

"Look, Watters," Bybee said. "We need to get something straight. I took on Sipes and the church for a reason, but that doesn't mean I'm ready to take on every damn lost cause there is, especially the way you want to take it on. And let's get something else straight. Reed told me why the last lawyer on this case quit. I may have left the church altogether, but that doesn't mean I'm going to sit here and listen to you bad-mouth Mormons."

Watters slowly squeezed his left eye shut and opened it, as if he were performing a facial exercise. "I haven't been bad-mouthing Mormons, my friend. And that's kind of odd, I mean, coming from a jack-Mormon, like you. But since we're straightening things out, let's get *this* straight. That last lawyer, Shields, was second chair—like you. I know that you've got ten times the experience I've got, and that you've tried a hundred more cases than I have, and that you were—are—one of the best criminal lawyers in Utah. I respect that; I respect you. But you're second chair. Boom. That's that. I know it's fucked, but there's nothing either one of us can do about it."

Bybee had been sitting, his coffee cup raised halfway to his mouth, frozen, listening, and now he set it on the table. "So what are you saying?"

"I'm saying that I'm calling the shots. And one of them is that I think Parks has been set up, and it's something to do with this Daughter of Zion." He leaned closer. "C'mon, Brig. I've heard you like to glide, so just glide, go with it."

Bybee shook his head. "With what? A conspiracy theory?"

"Yeah."

"Lord."

Watters paused, fiddling with his cup, as though he were stalling, letting the dust and smoke clear. "Look, man," he finally said, "Farnsworth had a granddaughter, a woman named Zolene Swapp." He smiled, his teeth easing out of his mouth. "Hear she's a looker. Anyway, they say she was real close to Farnsworth, his favorite, the only person he really cared about, confided in—shit like that. I want to talk to her."

"Well, you're calling the shots," Bybee said.

"She lives out of town, but they say she's coming in the day after tomorrow."

"*They* say?"

"Okay, my *source* says. A guy named Lloyd Honey, runs a service station here, sells a little beer, too. But I also got my investigator in Ogden working on this." Watters straightened his legal pad and plucked a cheap ballpoint pen out of his shirt pocket. "I need your phone number. Where are you staying?"

"In a tepee at the edge of town. Where are *you* staying?"

Watters pointed past Bybee, out the window. "Across the street at that Parry Lodge. All that dead movie star shit. The Barry Sullivan Room, whoever he was." He clicked the point out on his pen. "Seriously, Brig, where are you staying?"

"In a tepee. Seriously. The Piute Village—Villa. I don't know the number."

truding mouth, the hair at his throat, the god-awful happy-face shirt. He had suddenly become transfixed by it all, by the fact that he sat second chair to a wild-eyed conspiracy nut who was dredging up ghosts and demons, dreaming of a witch hunt. He coughed, righting himself, and dramatically looked at his watch; he had nowhere to go, nothing to do. "I've got to run."

He slid out of the seat and, as he stood up, caught a glimpse of himself in a mirror across the room. With his oiled black hair, his pleated slacks, and the white shirt with its rolled-up sleeves, he looked like someone who could well have been part of the "dead movie star shit" across the street—Robert Taylor maybe, or even Gilbert Roland. All he needed was a thin mustache and a wide-brimmed hat—maybe flatten the stomach a bit, lose the glasses.

He turned back to Watters, who had stayed seated and was doodling on his yellow legal pad. "You know," Bybee said, "trying a murder case is not some crazy detective movie that you write a script to as you go along."

"Yeah?" Watters said. "Then what is it?"

Bybee placed his fingers on the table, splayed, the thumbs touching, his hair dripping across his forehead. He had given this particular bit of advice before, many times; it was like a mantra, something always chanted throughout his life, muted, in the background.

"It's like riding a raft over a waterfall. You just hold on and hope for the best at the bottom."

Watters laughed and dropped the pen back in his pocket. "You're a real philosopher, Brig, but I like that movie thing the best. You know, we're just making this up as we go along." Watters's expression changed, and he winked. "By the way, how did the town of Beaver get its name?"

"It's not a town, Watters. It's a city."

"Okay, a city. And call me Ronnie."

"So long," Bybee said.

"Later."

Bybee walked away from the man and, halfway across the

Bybee walked away from the man and, halfway across the café, saw their waitress suddenly curse under her breath and begin hurrying toward the booth he had just left. He turned around and saw that Watters had lit a cigarette, his face nearly obscured by smoke, only his teeth and one eye visible.

3

BEGINNING in the Paunsaugunt Plateau, a terracework of cliffs slopes southward across Utah over the deep canyons and shallow streams of old Piute lands—pink cliffs above gray cliffs, gray cliffs above white, white above red—to form what some call the Grand Staircase. And it *is* a staircase, of sorts, a huge, sandstone thing where a monstrous god may have once clumped up to his celestial kingdom, or where invisible spirit babies may have tumbled downward into mortal life.

At its earthly end, this stairway stops at a place called Hell's Bellows, a slice of southern Utah where the winds forever blow, up and back, through the Vermilion Cliffs, the last tier.

Wedged back among those cliffs, in Johnson Canyon, sits a house, alone in the center of a scattering of dead fields and broken machines, alone in silence. Except for its right angles, the house is a natural part of the canyon, like an outcropping of chiseled and layered stone. Tall trees surround it, stretching their arms across the roof to shade it, to shield it, to enfold it into the vast sheeting of red, the endless whispering of death.

At a bend near a collapsed silo, she could see the house about a quarter of a mile away across the dead alfalfa fields and the gullies full of weeds and sage. And she saw a car—a car that should not be there—a white, angular thing parked among the rusted humps of abandoned machines. She quickly drove her Mustang to the end of the road, and at a black, gummy pond, she turned and roared through the sand and into the yard.

Watters stood on the cement back porch of the house, a yellow legal pad in his hand. He was dressed in jeans and a white short-sleeved shirt, and his jogging shoes were already dusted with red.

"Hey, hello," he yelled. He raised the legal pad like a signal flag, as though he were guiding the Mustang in.

The woman parked in the shade of a cottonwood tree and switched the engine off. She sat for a moment, and the dappling of shade and light seemed to camouflage her inside the car, but then she opened the door and got out. She was tall and slender, dressed in jeans and a loose, scoop-necked T-shirt that read "U of A" on the front, and she wore a pair of large sunglasses. She did not speak but only shook out her long hair, which in the bright sun seemed to flame up, burning, as red and brilliant as the cliffs around her.

"Hello," Watters said again, and he showed his teeth.

The woman still said nothing. She limped around the rear of the car and up to the edge of the porch, where she stopped, took off her sunglasses, and hooked them on her shirt collar.

Watters stood, paralyzed, realizing the talk in town was true—she was a beautiful woman. Her face was as white as paper, lightly freckled, with high cheekbones and crow-footed blue eyes that made her look like a countrified model.

"My name is Zolene Swapp," she said.

Watters continued to stare at her. She wore no lipstick, no rouge, no eyeliner, and except for a pair of dangling silver-and-turquoise earrings, no jewelry. He glanced at her left hand. She wore no rings.

"I'm Ronnie Watters," he said, and he thrust out a big hand.

Zolene took his hand, but rather than shake it, she gripped it tight and pulled herself up and onto the porch. She was annoyed; she had been driving all day and had looked forward to relaxing in this quiet place, alone. But now she had to contend with this man, and she pushed both of her hands into the back pockets of her jeans and examined him, as if wondering just what sort of odd specimen of life he was.

"I'm a lawyer," Watters said, and he took a business card from his shirt pocket and handed it to her. "I represent a man named Owen Parks. He's been charged with—"

"Murdering my grandfather," she said. She put the card in her back pocket without reading it. In front of her, the red hills almost shimmered in the bright sun, and the silence and solitude of the old place rose up, almost palpable. It was a place that had always been inviolate, secluded, removed from the rest of the world.

"How long have you been here?" she said. Her lips formed a natural moue, the upper lip raised in a faint pout.

"Oh, about thirty minutes." He lied; he had been waiting for her, pacing on the small porch, for over three hours. "The gates were open."

"There are no gates. You shouldn't be here."

"Look, I'm sorry about your grandfather, ma'am," he said. "I am. But I was appointed to this case. The trial starts in ten days. I just need to ask a few questions, if you don't mind."

Zolene turned and limped to the edge of the porch. She looked out at the leaning barn, the sagging fences, the heaps of machinery that had collapsed decades ago—an engine seized, an axle dropped—lying about like scattered corpses.

"Jeez, he's dead," she said. "Just leave him alone."

"Well, I understand; I'll be out of your hair real quick." He stopped and, as if taking the expression literally, looked at the red hair that flowed down her back, imagining himself entangled in it. "I just need to know a few things."

"Like what?"

"Well, who owns this place now?"

"I don't know. Look, I really—"

"What do you mean, you don't know?"

She stopped and looked him, at his cheap, plastic pen poised over the yellow pad, his head thrust forward. "Just what I said: I don't know. I really don't want to talk to you."

"Well," Watters said, "I guess you don't have to. But then I'll just subpoena you to the trial." He winked. "Catch you off guard, there."

Zolene studied the man again. He looked like a caricature of the persistent reporter or detective, dogged and snooping, and she knew he was serious with the threat. She could either talk to him here, on her own turf, or sit in a witness box at trial.

"Okay," she said.

"Good," Watters said. "You live here?"

"No, I live in Tucson. I'm here for the trial and to take care of a few things." She pointed north, at another house about half a mile away, partially hidden behind a grove of Russian olive trees, the only other house in the canyon. "Wester Lewis over there has been taking care of Doug's—my grandfather's—dog. Its name is Max. Wester says Max stays here all day, waiting for Doug to come back, I guess. I need to find him and take him into town, maybe back home, before he goes feral."

Watters clicked his pen and grinned. "Lewis or the dog?"

Zolene turned away and looked at the road that circled the house. It had been gouged out by years of trucks and cars grinding around it, and now it was like a moat, separating the two of them on the porch from the dead machines half buried in the sand, in the past.

"How long did he live here?" Watters said.

"Since the war—the end of the war."

"Vietnam War?"

She turned back around. "World War *Two*."

"Oh, okay," Watters said. He was oddly bent, scribbling on the pad that he propped against his thigh. "He live alone?"

"Yes . . . well, no. His wife, my grandmother—Myrna—lived with him, but she died in the late sixties."

"Okay." Watters continued writing, but the legal pad slipped and fell to the dusty porch. "Do you think we could go inside?" he said.

Zolene shook her head. After the funeral, she and her two young daughters had spent several days cleaning the place, restoring it after someone had virtually turned it upside down, every drawer and cupboard emptied. She wanted no more intruders; she did not even want to go inside, now, herself.

"No," she said. "Sorry."

She shoved her hands into her back pockets again and leaned back, stretching her shirt over her breasts, and Watters stared at them.

"Are you sleeping here?" he said. "Staying here, I mean?"

"No. In town, with my aunt. This place doesn't have water anymore. Cistern's dry."

"That's serious," he said, unsure just what a cistern was. He began to ask for her address, or a phone number, but he knew she would refuse. It was a small town, anyway; he could find her. He reached inside his shirt pocket and brought out his pack of Marlboros. "You mind if I smoke?"

"Yes," she said. "I do."

Watters dropped the cigarettes back in his pocket. "Okay. Just testing. Did you spend a lot of time here?"

"Yeah," she said. "Every summer. I helped Doug work the place."

Watters looked out over the tumbledown yard, the crumbling spread of rust and rot. "Okay." He stared at her. "You must like it out here?"

"Yes, I do."

"Why?"

"Well, that's none of your business, Mr. Watters. But mainly because it's private. At least it was."

The gibe glanced off him. "You knew him pretty well, you think? Your grandfather?"

Zolene didn't answer. No one, in the end, knew her grandfather; no one knew exactly why, over the years, he had let his ranch turn to red dust; why, toward the end, he had withdrawn from the world, cursing it; and why he had lived the last few years the way Wester Lewis had found him in death: alone and cold, curled in on himself.

"Yeah, I knew him," she finally said.

"He have any enemies? Anyone who would want to—?"

"No."

Watters cleared his throat and then rubbed the clump of hair just below it. "This may sound strange, but there's a rumor around town that Farns—your grandfather—may have been killed by something called the Daughter of Zion. You know anything—"

"The what?" She had a sudden vision of a gaggle of old women sitting around her grandfather's corpse in a drone of creaking voices, knitting, laughing.

"The Daughter of Zion."

"I've never heard of it."

"It was a Mormon secret police, a posse," Watters said, and he waited, expectant, like a boy who has just whispered an obscenity.

Zolene shook her head. Growing up in Kanab and on the ranch, she had heard of something called the Nauvoo Legion, some kind of Mormon standing army that never made it out west, but never of this.

"Never heard of it," she said again.

Watters took a step closer to her. He had driven to St. George earlier that morning, about an hour and a half away, to the library there, and done some research. Now he flipped some pages on the yellow pad and read what he had scribbled there.

"They were called lots of things: Sons of Dan, Danites, Thrasher . . ." He trailed off, his eyes wide, the way they must have been when Lloyd Honey, at the Texaco station in town, first told him the rumor. "They were formed back in Joseph Smith's day to—" He looked up. "Joseph Smith was the first—"

"I *know* who Joseph Smith was, Mr. Watters."

"Okay." He bent back to his notes. He had assumed she was LDS, but as he had done with the cigarettes, he was just testing. "Anyway," he said, "they were formed to protect the church, the Prophet, to go after anyone that tried to hurt them." He squinted at his own writing. "Blood atonement, it was called. Eye for an eye stuff. Anyway, they came out here from back East with the Mos—" He raised his head. "Sorry—*Mormons*. They came to Salt Lake. The Daughter of Zion was Brigham Young's private thugs, his muscle." He nodded. "That's a fact."

"Brigham Young's been dead a hundred years."

"I know, but they were supposed to protect him, any prophet, I guess, and all the Mormon settlers out here."

"Well, they didn't do a very good job last Thanksgiving."

Watters made a weak laugh and consulted his notes again. "They also went after—*apostates*. I think that's how you say it. Members of the church who were enemies, I guess. Deserters." He snorted. "Bunch of *mean* bastards." He looked helplessly at her. "Sorry."

Zolene stared at the cement, angry. Everywhere in Mormon country, even at its fringes in Tucson, Gentiles—non-Mormons like Watters—were always hammering away at the church, threatening to reveal horrors and hobgoblins and secret voodoo rituals that would convince the world of what they had been claiming for years: Mormonism was one big, scary cult.

"That's crap," she said.

Watters smiled. "Maybe not."

"Jeez," she said, and she turned away from him again.

Watters flipped several pages on his legal pad, all of them filled with his childish handwriting. "Okay. Anyway, so you don't know anyone who would have done something like this? I mean, murder your grandfather."

"No," she said. "Just your client."

"Well, that's—"

"I hope they hang his ass," she said.

She kept her back to him, and Watters took the opportunity to study her body—the narrow waist, the jeans stretched tight over her round buttocks, the long legs. He slowly closed one eye, as if taking aim. She was an incredible creature.

"Well, I understand," he finally said. "Anyway, this is not a death penalty case." He paused and then laughed. "If it was, he'd get his choice: firing squad or the needle. Law of the land."

Zolene turned around. "That's real neat, Mr. Watters."

"Call me Ronnie. Anyway, did your grandfather have anything out here on the ranch, anything valuable, something that someone would want pretty bad?"

"Like what?"

"Oh, I don't know." He looked above him as if words and ideas were floating in the air. "Jewelry, cash?"

"No."

"A coin collection? Gold doubloons?" He showed his teeth. "The gold plates?"

"No, and that's not very funny."

"Maybe something—anything—to do with the church?"

Zolene looked beyond him at a crescent-shaped butte about a mile away, one her grandfather had named "Dishpan." Years ago, inside the house, as she played on the living room rug under the high, cedarwood ceiling, she had heard them, the voices—Doug's and Carl's and her father's—deep, loud, demanding voices that slid horizontally across the room in layers, until her father nearly yelled.

"Damn it, Doug! Give it to the church."

Zolene shook her head and stuffed her hands into the back pockets of her jeans again. "No," she said.

"You don't think anything was taken from the house?"

"No. It was hard to tell, really. Everything was torn apart."

"No big, dark secrets?"

"What do you mean?"

Watters pointed at the other house in the canyon. "Wester Lewis over there told me that, three days before Thanksgiving Day, your grandfather left; he drove somewhere." He looked around him and then pointed at a green pickup truck coated in red dust. "In that. He didn't come back till Thanksgiving morning. Maybe with someone else. He was killed that afternoon."

"So?"

"So, where did he go?"

"I don't know."

Watters showed his teeth. "You sure?"

Zolene still had the letter Doug had mailed to her just before Thanksgiving, a long agonizing thing in his cramped script that she had tucked away in a drawer at home. It was the last thing he had ever written.

"I'm sure."

"He owed quite a bit of money, didn't he?" Watters said. "Banks calling in a loan or two?"

"No."

"You sure?"

"Yes."

Watters swatted at a fly with his legal pad. He seemed to be stalling, and he shifted his weight from one foot to the other.

"What do you know about the Mountain Meadows Massacre?" he said. Lloyd Honey had mentioned the words—almost whispered them—but it made little sense to him.

Zolene looked away; she seemed uncomfortable. "About what everyone else knows: nothing."

Watters waited, expecting her to wrinkle her face, puzzled over his last question. When she did not react, he pretended to study his notes, and then looked up.

"Well, that's about it. You've got my card, and I'm staying at that weird Parry Lodge in town—all that western movie star business." He stopped and looked out over the canyon, frowning, as if a band of black-hatted outlaws were thundering their way, trailed by a camera crew. "You ever heard of Barry Sullivan?"

"Yes."

He shrugged. "Huh. I've never heard of half these guys. Anyway, give me a call there if you think of anything important."

"What do you consider important?"

Watters laughed and shoved out his hand, and she quickly shook it and pulled back. "Well," he said, "I can tell you." He looked nervously around him, as though there were spies crouching in the sage, listening. "But not here. There's a pretty good restaurant in town called Chef's Palace. I mean, considering where we are, and all. I've got a dozen more questions for you. You want to meet me there tonight? Around seven?"

"You asking me for a date?"

His teeth seemed to pop out, one by one. "Yeah, I guess so. You want to go?"

"No."

"Okay." He flushed and looked out over the red sand and red cliffs, at the dry, airless, alien look of it all. "You know," he said, "sometimes I think that I've landed on Mars."

"Maybe you have," Zolene said.

He looked at her eyes, as blue and hard as the sky overhead, and then hopped off the porch and walked to his car. For a moment, under the bright sun, his white shirt seemed to merge with his white car, melting together into a radiance, and then he opened the door and got in. Zolene followed, limping, pulling her left leg in front of her so that it skimmed across the sand.

Watters watched her struggle across the yard. He had thought, earlier, that the problem was temporary, a sore muscle or a cramp from the long drive, but he realized that she had a bona fide dead leg, a true limp.

She came up to the open window, placed her hands on either side, and leaned her face in. "Why would Parks take a picture of him, Mr. Watters?"

As she bent to speak to him, her shirt, weighted by the sunglasses, had gapped down, and Watters slightly craned his neck so as to better stare at her bra, easily visible, and the tops of her breasts. "What makes you think Parks took that picture? And call me Ronnie. Later."

He started the engine, put the car in gear, and pulled away from her. He drove slowly around the house, and then crept by the black pond and accelerated when he was out on the road. Like a sentinel, Zolene stood and watched the car bump along in front of the red hills, pink dust boiling up behind it, until it disappeared near the collapsed silo.

She fished Watters's card from his back pocket and rubbed her thumb over it, the way her late husband had once taught her, to see if it was engraved. It wasn't; it was printed—cheaply, at that—and she jammed it back into her pocket.

She limped across the deep sand to a fence that leaned toward the ground, and stepped over it into the corral. An old black Plymouth sedan sat parked there in the weeds as though her grandfather had left it running while he popped into the barn, and then had forgotten it—for forty years.

She cupped her hands to her mouth. "Max!" she yelled.

She moved past the car and into the barn. It was immense, and the sun shooting through scores of holes in the roof filled the dark place with slanting shafts of white, like a photograph of sleet. She moved deeper inside. The place smelled of mice and damp wood and mold, and big yellow loops of baling twine still hung from posts by the stalls, tossed there after she or Doug or one of the Navajo hands had cracked open a bale of hay.

"Max!" she shouted again, and then waited, listening.

She walked back outside and, after poking around some sheds and horse stalls, limped down a short road studded with Russian thistle. At the road's end, in the middle of a weedy apple orchard, sat another house, this one made of brick and petrified wood. It was abandoned, ruined, smothered in the dense foliage, and everything—the yard and the house, even the air—was dark; it had always been dark.

She limped into the orchard and stopped near the house. "Max!"

Only a few hundred yards away, on the other side of a deep gulch, was a line of low cliffs, and she waited, half expecting an echo from them, but the canyon swallowed the sound whole. She began to turn around, to return to the sunlight, when she saw the dog. It was in the shadows, hanging from one of the apple trees by its neck, its once big gray body shriveled and collapsed.

She screamed—a high yelp, like a bark—and then saw the man standing by the old house, only ten yards away. He was an Indian, in dirty pants and a checkered shirt, and his face was dark, glistening. He grinned and showed a missing tooth.

Zolene pivoted and tried to run toward the other house, back into the sunlight and down the road, but her foot dragged through the weeds so that she only lurched just faster than a walk. She finally stumbled to the road and stopped and looked over her shoulder, expecting the Indian to be closing, his thick body rushing through the thistle toward her.

But he had turned and was running the other way. His long hair bounced as he loped heavily across the dry fields toward the cliffs where a pickup truck was parked on a dirt road.

Her hands shaking, Zolene watched the man disappear into the gulch and, a moment later, emerge on the other side, climb into his truck, and drive away.

Within seconds, the truck vanished into the gathering blackness of the canyon, the growl of its engine finally silent.

4

ON a summer night in 1943, about a dozen Kanab men—all non-Mormons—crouched together in the darkness. They were observing the annual Moccasin Watermelon Days ritual, and as that event demanded, they were dressed as Indians: watercolor war paint, feathers, and loincloths made from their wives' kitchen towels.

They laughed and shoved each other and then clambered into cars and drove across the state line to the grasslands south of Milt's Tavern—now called the Buckskin Tavern. There, drinking bad whiskey and eating watermelon and venison jerky, they whooped around a bonfire, happy.

But around midnight, when they were at full drunken throttle, a crippled B-25 on a training mission droned unevenly overhead. One by one, the crew bailed out, and the men around the bonfire watched the parachutes blossom in the darkness and float downward.

Howling, full of patriotic fire, the Watermelon Indians went crashing across the landscape to rescue their countrymen. But when two of the bomber's crew, safely on the ground, saw the screaming savages advancing on them, they turned tail and ran.

Across the ravines and the clumps and sage and the tiny mesas they stumbled, never looking back, until they arrived at the only light in the night, the only sign of civilized life: Milt's Tavern.

They burst into the bar in their leather headgear and baggy flight suits and pointed frantically behind them.

"Indians!" one of them yelled. "Holy Jesus . . . *Indians*!"

The sun was hovering over Kanab's western hills when Zolene roared up to the intersection at Lloyd Honey's Texaco, where a big overhead sign directed tourists south, to the Grand Canyon. She drove through the red light, turned north down Center Street, and raced into the middle of town.

As she had done twice during the furious ten-minute drive in from the ranch, she tried to contact the sheriff's department on her cell phone, but was met again with the bleating busy signal.

"Damn it," she said.

For a moment, she considered driving directly to the sheriff's department, but she knew that the persistent signal on their phone did not mean that Lamar or his deputy was "busy" but, simply, that they refused to answer—and would probably refuse to help. Besides, in addition to being dirty and tired and frightened out of her wits, she was hungry, so just past an intersection everyone called Big Joe's Junction, she pulled up and parked in front of the church, just behind a tilting RV. When the traffic cleared, she got out and limped across the street to the Trail's End, but the pimply-faced girl with the cowboy hat and six-gun met her at the door.

"War full up," the girl said.

"You seen Lamar Little?" Zolene said. "The sheriff?"

"No."

"LeGrand? His—"

"No."

Zolene turned around and stood stupidly on the sidewalk. "Damn it," she said again.

She walked up the street, past the Book Outpost, to the Pow-Wow, a big souvenir store and café made to look like an old trading post. In front, on a creaking porch, a wooden Indian stood atop a tree stump, staring out over the street with painted eyes. One hand was upraised in peace, but the thumb and forefinger had been broken off, creating a lopsided Boy Scout salute.

She stood for a moment staring at the Indian, and briefly

considered driving to her aunt's house and digging out the bottle of Scotch she knew the woman kept in the pantry, behind the olive oil and cooking sherry and homemade root beer.

But she pushed open the door and walked in. Most of the place was filled with shelves of tourist fare, and dozens of foreigners in sandals and odd-colored pants were shuffling around, trying on vests and hats and turquoise jewelry. In the rear was an old-fashioned lunch counter, complete with chromed and padded stools, and Zolene walked to it. There was only one vacant seat, at the very end, next to a man with dark hair who was hunched over a cup of coffee, and she plopped down, exhausted. She rested her hands on the counter, but when she saw that they were still trembling, she folded them into her lap.

"Jeez," she mumbled to herself.

The dark-haired man next to her raised his head. It was Bybee, and he put down his coffee cup and turned toward her. "I'm sorry?"

Zolene shook her head, embarrassed, and looked at the countertop. "No. I mean, I was just . . . talking to myself."

Bybee smiled, his eyes softening. "Talking's okay. Just don't *argue* with yourself."

Zolene nodded at him, relieved when he turned back to his coffee. While she waited, she swiveled on her stool, and through a long, narrow window in the rear surveyed the Pow-Wow's phony frontier town built in back. It had false-fronted stores, a blacksmith shop, hitching posts, and in the middle of the dirt street, a wooden gallows with a dangling rope noose. It was all part of the grand shoot-'em-up melodrama that the Pow-Wow presented now and then for the busloads of tourists.

A waitress in a pink-and-white smock came up to her. "Hey, Zolene. How you doin'?"

Zolene swiveled back around and stared at her, trying to remember the woman's name. "I'm fine," she answered. She was aware of Bybee looking at her. "Let me have a tuna salad on toast and some iced tea."

"Okay," the waitress said. She hesitated, then cocked her

head and made a dismal face. "I'm shore sorry about your granddad. He's in our prayers. You, too."

"Thank you."

The waitress left and Zolene sat, struggling, still trying to dredge up the woman's name. She was one of the Chamberlain girls—she knew that—but there were five of them in town. She was either Norleen or Arletta, maybe Clytie Rae. . . .

"You're Zolene Swapp," Bybee said.

Zolene seemed startled, and she leaned right away from Bybee. In the mirror behind the counter, next to a board filled with Polaroid snapshots of the Pow-Wow employees, she looked at him. He didn't appear to be a local; he wore slacks and a button-down shirt and, unlike every man in town this time of year, he was not growing a beard. But he looked familiar, something about the deep eyes, the mouth.

"Yes," she said.

"Douglas Farnsworth's granddaughter?"

"Yes. Who are you?"

"My name is Brig Bybee." He nodded at the waitress, who was at the other end of the counter. "I'm sorry about your grandfather, too. I truly am."

Zolene looked at the familiar but unrecognizable face in the mirror. She felt as though she were swimming underwater in the lake just outside of town, the way they had done in high school on Ditch Day. She was gliding, her eyes open, but everything was shadowy and murky, even familiar faces of her friends next to her like ghosts . . . like floating corpses.

Then, as though surfacing into the daylight and clear air, she remembered, and she turned and addressed him in the flesh, not the mirror. "You're a lawyer."

Bybee laughed. "That obvious, huh?"

"The church thing. The rape case against Bellard Sipes. It was in the news, your picture and all."

"Yeah, that's me." He smiled, sadly, not sure whether to be flattered by the notoriety. "That *was* me."

"So how do you know my grandfather? And me?"

Bybee waited as the waitress set Zolene's iced tea and silverware in front of her and walked away. "I've been appointed to represent—to help represent—Owen Parks, the man who's—"

The deadness that was always in her leg seemed to rise, to grip the rest of her, numbing her, and she thought for an instant that she would be sick. She swayed there, and then suddenly waved her hand, angrily, as though swatting at a flying pest. "Another one. What do you guys do, take turns following me around?"

Bybee looked surprised. "I'm not following—"

"You know, I just stood out in the sun for an hour answering questions from another lawyer. A creepy guy named—" She stopped. She couldn't remember; she was underwater again, the world a jumble of nameless faces.

"Ronnie Watters?" Bybee said.

"Yeah. Watters. I've had all I want from him. All this weird stuff about secret police, something." She shook her head again. "God, I'm *sick* of it. I'm not answering any more questions."

"I don't want to ask you questions."

"Right. That's why you followed me here."

Bybee held his hands out, tanned and long-fingered, and Zolene stared at them. "Ms. Swapp, I didn't follow you here. If anything, you followed me."

Zolene blinked and stared at Bybee's reflection in the mirror. She realized how absurd the accusation was, how paranoid, and she suddenly felt weak, as though she hadn't slept in days. She closed her eyes; they felt raw and hot, and the image of the dead, rotted dog and the grinning Indian swam in front of her. The numbness still gripped her, and she swallowed, hard, and then barely had time to put one hand to her face before she choked and began crying.

Bybee immediately put one hand behind her back, as though she might crumple backward. "Are you okay?" he said. He looked scared, and he took her paper napkin that had been wrapped around the silverware and gave it to her.

Zolene took the napkin and cried into it in soft, rhythmic sobs. The waitress came up, her eyes wide, and looked helplessly at Bybee. "I shouldn't have said nothing."

"It's okay," Bybee said. He gently put his hand on Zolene's elbow and held her for a few seconds. "She'll be okay."

The woman seemed unsure, but she walked away, and Bybee lowered his head so he could look into Zolene's face. "Will you be okay?" he said.

Zolene had stopped crying, and now she sat, her head down as she dabbed at her eyes with the napkin. "Yes," she said in a whisper. "I think so."

"Can I get you anything? Call someone?"

"No." She sniffed and took a shuddering breath. "Thanks." She shook her head and her hair spilled in different directions. "It's just that—"

Bybee waited several beats. "That what?"

She took another deep breath and then straightened up and drank some of her iced tea. She felt somewhat composed now, although her blue eyes were still watery, and she turned to Bybee. Again, there was something familiar in his face, but it was a familiarity that was not derived from half-remembered newspaper photographs, from rumors or gossip. Rather, it was a maturity and kindness that was real, sitting before her, the type that she had once luxuriated in every day, one that she had once taken for granted. He was like Drew, she realized, a genuine human being—sympathetic and understanding, with a true sense of humor—and she needed all of that now, desperately. She needed to talk to Drew again.

So for the next few minutes, she told Bybee about the day, about the drive up from Tucson, the skirmishing with Watters, and then, beginning to cry again, about the horror of finding the dead dog and seeing the Indian leering at her.

Bybee handed her his own napkin. "Did you call the police?"

"No. Well, yes. They don't answer."

"Never one around when you need 'em."

For the first time since she had sat down, Zolene smiled. "I guess."

She examined his face again, the hooded eyes, the straight nose, the gentleness that seemed to reside there, the intelligence, even the suffering—all of it so familiar, so comfortable.

She suddenly felt a twinge of guilt, a sense of betrayal of the dead, opening up to this stranger in a way she had rarely done with any man since Drew had died. Without touching her, except for lightly taking hold of her elbow, he had held her in a way, embraced her, soothed her the way Drew used to soothe her.

She looked at Bybee and then at the mirror, at his reflection, and then back again, as if she were deciding between two different men.

"Look," she said. "I'm sorry about . . . jumping down your throat a few minutes ago. "It's just that when you said who you were—"

Bybee brightened. "Hey, I don't blame you. Two lawyers in one afternoon will ruin anyone's day. That's like two trips to the dentist."

"So true," she said, and her silver earrings bounced as she laughed, finally.

"Anyway," Bybee said, "I'll apologize for both of us." He could see, in his mind's eye, the man looming over her, his "comparative lunacy" strategy self-evident, made manifest. "For being in the middle of your life all of a sudden."

"Well, you certainly are."

Bybee froze, unsure of what she meant, and for an instant he thought that she would make an excuse, stand up and walk away, and a surge of panic caught at him.

"Hey," he said. He raised one hand, palm outward, like the wooden Indian outside, and cleared his hair from his face with the other. "Let's make a deal: We won't talk about Watters, about the case, about . . . any of that. Okay?"

Zolene shifted her eyes from the reflection back to him. There was a rational, reasonable part of her—something bright and humming that was fitted in her brain—that said she should not even wait for her sandwich, but simply mumble a good-bye and walk away. This man, after all, was defending the monster who put a bullet through Doug's brain. But there were other parts of her, the irrational and unreasonable—the fouled gears and frayed wires, like in those damned dead machines at the ranch—that kept her welded to the stool, kept her thinking about the past, that made her suddenly extend her hand to this man.

"Okay," she said, and she smiled as she thought of the old soothsayer's warning: *"You will meet a tall, dark . . ."*

Bybee put his hand in hers, and both of them gently gripped one another longer than a normal handshake would allow. A tangle of her red hair had fallen across her face, obscuring one eye, and he had to fight the temptation to reach out and smooth it back, the way he always smoothed his own.

"So, what do we talk about?" Bybee said.

Before she could answer, the waitress arrived with the sandwich on a plate, surrounded by a ring of broken potato chips. It had been cut diagonally, and Zolene, not as hungry as she had first believed, offered Bybee one half. He accepted, and for several seconds they ate in silence—she slowly, only nibbling, while Bybee devoured the sandwich like a hay baler. During it all, both of them stared awkwardly out the low window at the gallows.

Zolene put her sandwich down. "Can I ask you something, Mr. Bybee?"

"Sure, but call me Brig."

"Okay. That Sipes thing. Did you believe your client, the missionary girl? I forget her name."

"Becky," Bybee said. "Rebecca Chu."

"Chu," Zolene repeated. She took a bite of her sandwich and slowly worked at it, and Bybee braced himself. He expected, even from this woman, some joke, some adolescent wordplay, the way his friends had done back then: *"Becky Chu . . . but she don't swallow." "Becky Chu Yu, then Becky Sue Yu."* Something similar to that.

"I like that name," Zolene said. "Anyway, did you believe her?"

Bybee nodded. The Salt Lake jury had absorbed four solid days of wild testimony: the constant "chance" encounters between Becky and Sipes, the gifts, the flattery, the choice assignments around the temple grounds, the witnesses who actually saw them together. Then, clear evidence of Sipes—his tiny mouth set, his eyes like colorless marbles set into his face—closing in for the kill; his pawing at her, the forced oral sex, his ceaseless, brutal humping of the tiny, twenty-one-year-old Chinese-American. And then, when she finally and tearfully spilled it all to other church leaders, there came the threats, the countercharges—the lies. God, the lies.

"Yes," Bybee said. "I still do."

He waited; he knew that, if she believed he took on difficult, hopeless cases because of a true belief in the client, then the next logical question would be, Then you must believe in Owen Parks? But they had just struck a deal, and she sat silently, honoring it, slowly eating.

After a few moments she patted her mouth with a napkin. "Are you LDS?"

"Well, I was—sort of," Bybee said. "I was a jack-Mormon, but I dropped out altogether after the trial." He tried to laugh, but it sounded more like a gasp. "Dropped out of a lot of things."

"Like what?"

"Like my family."

Zolene looked horrified, her mouth open, her eyes widening. "Your *family*?"

"Yeah," Bybee said. "I'm . . . divorced." He paused, realizing that it was getting easier to use that word, to admit to it. He spread his hands out on the counter, palms up and empty, as if displaying his innocence, making the explanation easier. "My wife—ex-wife—Helena, is a good woman, dyed-in-the-wool Mormon, claims her ancestors came out here with Brigham Young, pulling a handcart. You know the story."

Zolene smiled. "Yes. I hear it a lot."

"Anyway, the church, the religion, has always been the most important thing in her life. My daughter's, too."

Zolene brightened. "You have a daughter? I have two daughters. What's her name?"

Bybee looked steadily at her, a faint smile on his face. "Brileena."

"Brileena," Zolene said. She seemed to be tasting it, her tongue working slowly in her mouth. "Brileena."

"Yeah," Bybee said. "Another goofy Mormon name, right? Sounds like a hair rinse?"

"Oh, no." Zolene reflexively begin to reach for his arm, to assure him, but stopped and placed her hand on the counter, instead. "It's a pretty name."

"Well, it's the Utah Mash. You know, forcing the parents' first names together: Brig-Helena. Brileena. It was the big thing back then."

"It's a pretty name," Zolene said again.

"I guess, but I fought it," Bybee said. "Like I did everything."

"What do you mean?"

"Oh, I don't know. My folks—rest their souls—were both card-carrying Mormons, and I was raised LDS; Helena and I were even married in the temple, in Manti, but—" He shrugged and looked helplessly at her.

"It wore off," she said.

"Some of it. Like I said, I was a jack-Mormon; I went on a toot now and then, raised a little hell. We were separated, once. I had a—" Again, he stopped, embarrassed.

"Fling? An affair?"

Bybee studied the woman for a moment, taking in the way she unconsciously leaned toward him, her blue eyes fastened on his face, carefully watching his mouth as if she were lip reading. She was interested—genuinely interested—and for the first time in several years, he felt comfortable with a woman, with another human being.

"Yeah," Bybee said. "A stupid affair. Anyway, like I was beginning to tell you, the church is the most important thing in Helena's life—Brileena's, too. It rises above everything. And I mean *everything*. So by the time the Sipes trial came along, things were getting pretty rocky with us. Then, after the trial, everything blew up and I became Satan incarnate—to her, to everyone."

"Just for suing Sipes?"

"Well, it wasn't just 'suing Sipes.' I sued a man who, someday down the line, will probably be the next prophet and president of the church. And I accused him of rape, of obstruction of justice, of lying, of being one of the most evil men on the face of the planet. And I accused the church itself, the First Presidency, the Quorum of the Twelve—hell, everyone—of concealing it all, of"—he shook his head, as if trying to rattle the next word out of his mouth—"*conspiracy*. They crucified me." He inwardly winced at his clashing metaphors, of Satan nailed to a cross.

"Were you excommunicated?"

"No, but they were thinking about it. I left of my own accord. I was already half out the door, anyway."

Zolene seemed relieved, and she leaned back. "That's good."

"That I left?"

"No. Well . . . yeah. I mean, you can always go back."

Bybee knew that the woman had to have been raised like Helena, like so many: the inveterate proselytizer, forever hopeful and forgiving. "Like leaving a movie?" he said. "I just keep my ticket stub so I can get back in?"

Zolene looked thoughtful. "You could say that."

"Well, I guess I can go back to the church if I want to. The problem is, I haven't found a reason to go back."

"I found one."

Bybee chuckled. "For me?"

"No, I mean, for me."

"Yeah?" He was relieved to shift the subject away from himself. "How so?"

Zolene signaled the waitress for a refill of her iced tea, and after she received it and sipped at it, she told Bybee some of her history. She had been born in Kanab, raised here within the bosom of a stout Mormon family, but like so many her age, left both the town and the church immediately after graduation. She ended up in Tucson at the University of Arizona and, continually drifting farther from her religion, fell in love with a Gentile, a man named Drew, ten years her senior. They were married, settled in Tucson—she a schoolteacher and he an engineer—and eventually had two girls. She became a modern woman, even retaining her maiden name, and the Mormon church and all of its rural, communal, teetotaling trappings were forever buried. At least, she thought they were.

"And then my husband was killed," she said. "We were coming back from a party. We had been drinking; Drew was drunk and he hit a guardrail and we flipped. He died instantly." She slapped her left leg. "And I got this."

Bybee did not understand the last remark, but he lowered his eyes. "I'm sorry," he said.

"So I was left to raise two little girls by myself. I still had some LDS friends, and I guess I turned to them by"—she shrugged—"I don't know . . . instinct. Like a reflex. I began going to church again, and it helped; it really helped."

"It does."

She didn't hear him. "You can say what you want about the church, Brig, but it concentrates on the home, on the kids. On raising kids. It got me back on track." She smiled. "I guess I'm kind of like you. I still drink now and then and cuss up a storm when I'm mad, so I guess that makes me a jack-Mormon, too."

"Jill-Mormon."

"Yeah," she said. "Anyway, despite that stuff, I realized that I had never really left the church; I just . . . I don't know."

"Went on sabbatical?" Bybee said.

"Yeah." Zolene raised her eyebrows. "Maybe you're just on sabbatical, too."

"Maybe."

"Anyway, the girls—Merideth and April—and I spent a lot of time up here, working the ranch with Doug. That helped, too. The girls are fine now. They're both in good schools, they play—"

Bybee nodded and smiled as he listened to Zolene prattle on about her daughters. He loved listening to her; he loved watching her mouth, the way it made the faint pout when she paused, the way her blue eyes seemed to dance along with the words. And he was nearly drunk with her hair, the way it glowed, even in this dim café, like woven strands of light. He could listen to her all night.

"I guess I should get going," Zolene said. She nodded out the window, where darkness was beginning to settle in on the phony frontier town, the tall gallows spooky and ominous in the half-light.

The earlier twinge of panic returned, and Bybee's mind began groping for some pretense to keep her seated, if even for a few minutes. "What are you going to do about the dog . . . in the orchard?"

Zolene's shoulders sagged. "Oh, jeez." She looked genuinely troubled, worn down. "I don't know."

"Look," Bybee said. "If you want, I can bury it for you. I imagine there's a shovel at the place. Just tell me how to get there. Directions."

"There are dozens of shovels," she said, and as she had done earlier, she gazed alternately between the flesh-and-blood Bybee and his reflection. The shining apparatus in her brain was screaming at a high-speed whine, the gauges redlined, but it made no difference. She stared for several moments into his eyes, luminous, alive, even behind the glasses. "Why don't you go out there with me? I can show you where Max is."

"Great," Bybee said.

"Got a pen?" She reached along the counter and found a clean paper napkin, and then took the ballpoint Bybee quickly produced. She scribbled her aunt's address and phone number—something she could not believe she was doing—and gave it to Bybee. "Tomorrow? About ten?"

"Great," Bybee said again. He inwardly winced, as he had done before, at his sudden ineptitude with words, his vocabulary reduced to one blurted syllable. He carefully folded the napkin and put it in his wallet.

Zolene swept up both of the receipts that the waitress had set down earlier, studied them, then dug into her front jeans pocket and pulled out a crumpled wad of bills. "I'll get it," she said, and she laid five dollars on the counter. "You can get the next one."

That promise was not lost on Bybee, and they both stood up together and he stepped back, allowing her to proceed in front of him. When Zolene took her first step, she lurched on her dead leg, and as he had done earlier, Bybee instinctively put out his hand to steady her. But then he remembered her slapping the leg, and he watched, unable to take his eyes off her as she limped through the store toward the front.

Zolene opened the door and walked out, but Bybee stopped next to a rack of disposable lighters to examine a display of post-cards, always opting to buy cards rather than take photographs. As he stood there, he looked up and, across the store, spotted the fat man he had seen in the back of the patrol car the day before. He was gray-haired and tall—as tall as Bybee, well over six feet—but his body seemed to begin at his ears and slope outward, a spreading mass of flesh that quivered to its limit at his belt and then curved back into his knees.

Zolene had not seen him; he had been sitting, concealed, Bybee guessed, in a small alcove where tourists were trying on cowboy boots, and he had probably been watching the two of them talk for some time. Now he stood in the doorway to the alcove, blocking it, and he stared hard at Bybee, his bearded face bloated and heavy.

Bybee turned and left the store and came up to Zolene on the sidewalk. It was dark now, the air cooling fast, and across Center Street, the lights of the church had come on, making it nearly blaze.

"Oh, God," Zolene said, and she pointed across the street at the church. "Look."

Bybee squinted into the darkness and saw Watters leaning on the fender of a Mustang, a glowing cigarette dangling out of his mouth. He looked like a high school punk, his head cocked, his hands thrust in his pockets. He spotted them, and he grinned and waved.

"He knows my car," Zolene said. "He's been waiting for me."

Bybee considered sending her back into the Pow-Wow, both to shield her from Watters and to satisfy her earlier need to contact the police. But the huge, blubbery man in the gray uniform who lurked inside seemed sinister, more a threat than a refuge.

"Just wait here," Bybee said, and he took her elbow again

and pulled her to the side, so that she stood next to the wooden Indian. "I'll talk to him."

With long, purposeful strides, Bybee crossed the street and came up to Watters, who smiled at him through a haze of cigarette smoke.

"Hey, studly," Watters said, "that's pretty quick work. Little young for you, though. I figure she's thirty-five, thirty-eight, max."

Behind them, at the entrance to the church, was a circle of illuminated display cases, each showing a poster of one of the Mormon icons—Moroni, Smith, others—including a painting of God and Jesus, both identically robed and bearded, both with identical American faces.

"Why don't you leave her alone?" Bybee said. His thin face was hard, set, his jaw muscles working.

Watters straightened from his slouch and stood face-to-face with Bybee, the cigarette still plugged into his mouth. "Well, I don't see your brand on her, my friend. Least, not the last time I looked."

"She doesn't like you."

Watters blew a stream of smoke out the side of his mouth. "Well, maybe she just doesn't know me."

"She does. Stay away from her."

"Or you'll do what? Challenge me to a duel?" He laughed and then his face changed in an instant, like a plastic Cracker Jack toy that's tilted one way or another. "Look, lover boy, in case you've forgotten, we're defending a murder case, and that woman"—he jabbed his cigarette across the street at Zolene—"is a witness."

"Lord. Witness to what?"

"A lot. I've been sniffing around. Something weird was going on in Farnsworth's life just before he was killed, and that little bitch knows what it was."

"Watch your mouth."

Watters tiredly shook his head. "Listen. She told me this afternoon that she doesn't know who owns that ranch now. But I already checked that out a week ago. The old man left *her* the property—the whole shebang. He changed his will a couple of years ago and didn't leave his son shit. Farnsworth also owed a pile of money, which she denied."

"So what does that prove?"

"Not much, other than she's lying her nice little round ass off." Watters blew another jet of smoke out and grinned. "You've noticed that, I'm sure. Her ass, I mean."

Bybee took a deep breath and moved a half-step backward. "Look, she's upset, confused."

"Maybe not." Watters looked at the woman across the street. "She a Mo?"

"Does it matter?"

"Yeah, it does. I'm getting the idea that this whole case is soaked in Mormon shit, top to bottom. You can smell it." He waved his hand at Zolene, dismissing her. "Anyway, fuck her. I want you to come with me to the jail tomorrow to see our pal Parks. You need to meet him."

"Fuck *him*," Bybee echoed.

"Fine. You don't want to work this case, I'll let Mackleprang know. Then he lets the state bar know." He dropped the cigarette and ground it out with his heel. "They don't really like you up there." He winked. "Like I say, I've been sniffing around."

As it had done in the judge's office the other day, the hot flush of mortification drained from Bybee's head down into his stomach. Mackleprang, and now this arrogant prick, were blackmailing him, threatening him with his own law license.

"I'm going to give Parks a little quiz tomorrow," Watters said. "A test. I want you to see it." He twisted his body around and looked at the clock on the church. When he straightened up, his face had changed and his voice was lower, friendlier. "But now, my friend, I'm going to go get drunk. There's a pretty good bar outside of town, across the line. Buckskin Tavern. Decent beer, not too many Navs. You interested?"

For a fleeting, delicious second, the prospect of a drink *did* interest Bybee, but it was the bottle—the languishing and laughing in the bottom of it—that had landed him in front of this lout.

"No," Bybee said.

"Ah, hell." Watters looked sad, defeated. "Anyway, meet me at the jail tomorrow at one. After feeding." He pointed to the southwest. "It's just over there. Follow the grid; you'll find it."

The humiliation of being ordered about by Watters was more than Bybee could endure, and he resolved, at that moment, that he would not do it. He would refuse; he would file the paperwork necessary tomorrow to remove himself from the case, and then confront Mackleprang and the state bar and whatever career-ending calamity might descend.

But then he turned around and looked at Zolene standing on the Pow-Wow porch, her beautiful face averted, as though she refused to watch. He stared down Center Street, at the tourists scuttling from their silvery buses to their motel rooms, settling in for several nights' stay. They all had a reason to be here, even if it was transient and temporary, and he looked back at Zolene. She was watching him now, and she shook her hair out of her face.

"Okay," Bybee said. "I'll be there."

5

ONE of the things that Bybee liked about Utah was that all of its communities, big and small, were built upon the Plat of Zion, the so-called Mormon grid that Smith or Young—or some Saint—had envisioned for the new kingdom on earth, the New Jerusalem. All of the streets were wide—too wide, really—and they all ranged out in perfect, right-angled, north-south symmetry from the spiritual and social and, arguably, *business* epicenter of the community: the church. And each street was given a military-style designation based upon its relative direction and distance from the chapel—300 north or 400 west.

It was a clever plan, Bybee always argued, that allowed all the drop-outs and deadbeats and jack-Mormons and Jill-Mormons to navigate their way back to the church, staggering, sobbing for forgiveness.

The sheriff's office in Kanab was located at 108 South, 200 West—on the first block south and two blocks west of the church—and after leaving Zolene at her aunt's house, Bybee drove his Toyota there along the grid.

The one-story brown brick building was built on what had once been a residential street, a cluster of old houses now converted to struggling businesses gathered under big elms and cottonwoods. But the county, to convince the locals that this was indeed the government and not some mom-and-pop enterprise like its neighbors, had chopped down all the trees on its property, front, side, and back. Now the sheriff's office, and the older, sandstone jail behind it, sat in a bright, dried-out square of land, a plot of authoritarian sunlight.

As he expected, Watters was waiting for him in front, smoking a cigarette as he paced along the sidewalk. He was dressed in white tennis shoes, navy blue slacks, and a white, short-sleeved shirt with military-style epaulets. He waved a manila folder as Bybee parked and exited the car.

The sight of Watters—boorish, grinning, dressed like a military school cadet, and seemingly oblivious to the instant bad blood between the two of them—had a leaden effect on Bybee, especially after the delicious morning he had spent.

As he and Zolene had arranged, he had gone to her aunt's house that morning, and the two of them had driven to the Farnsworth ranch, a pleasant ten-minute ride east of town. Once there, Zolene, still refusing to enter her grandfather's house, showed him the rest of the place: the barn, some old horse stalls, and finally the abandoned house in the orchard where the dog still hung. While she stood some distance away, her back turned, Bybee cut the poor creature down and buried it. It was wretched work; the dog was like a greasy, stinking rug, and digging the grave with the rusted shovel proved a tougher chore than he had imagined.

But he didn't care. If they had stood over the rotted carcass of the dog all morning or he had dug a hundred graves, it would have been fine with him. Zolene—fresh and sweet-smelling, her hair glinting like red foil—was one of the most hypnotizing women he had ever met, and the few hours spent talking and strolling with her around the wrecked place had been heady, like a dream.

"Hey, studly," Watters yelled. He came up to Bybee and gave him a glancing slap on the back. "You ready to rock and roll?"

Bybee, dressed in black loafers, gray slacks and a dark knit shirt, inspected the other man's strange outfit. "Your commanding officer know you're here?"

Watters laughed and then pointed at Bybee. "Your foursome know *you're* here?"

Bybee did not return the laugh, and the two of them walked to the front of the sheriff's office and went inside. Like most offices, it smelled of air-conditioning and carpet cleaner, but behind it, like a stain that couldn't be washed away, was another odor, maybe the dank smell of government, of old ledgers and disinfectant, of bureaucracy gone to seed, something indefinable.

"Smells like shit," Watters said.

A matronly woman in a plain dress and thick shoes greeted them. She had a chrome badge that said "Marla Hamblin" pinned on her blouse, riding atop big, heavy breasts that ached toward the floor. She told them to have a seat, and they sat down in unsteady, plastic chairs.

Watters turned to Bybee. "See her?" he whispered. "Bet she's only twenty-eight or so. Thirty, max. Looks forty-five, though."

"Maybe," Bybee said.

"Maybe, hell. Look at those tits. She was probably a looker, once, but the Body Snatchers got her."

Bybee squinted at him, his thick eyebrows almost touching. "What are you talking about?"

"The Mos got her," Watters said. "You never seen that movie? You nod off; you drop your guard and—*wham*! The Body Snatchers got you. It's called conversion, my friend."

Annoyed, Bybee turned away and watched the woman as she puttered around the office. As much as he hated to admit it to himself, Watters was probably right. He had touched upon a theme that had always disturbed him: the church's heavy-handed sexist treatment—or just plain ignorance—of women. The secretary, Marla, was pretty, but he knew the church had transformed her, blunted her, forced her into fleshy, premature homeliness. Like Brileena, his own daughter, the instant they emerged from the mysterious ceremony, long underwear—the holy garments—itching under wedding dresses, they began to change. Slim bodies became bloated, bright eyes turned sad and dull, hair thinned and pulled itself back, the gait slowed, and backs suddenly hunched. They were pod people, shape-shifters, something, as Watters claimed, from a science fiction movie.

But Zolene had evaded it—somehow.

A door behind the woman opened, and a uniformed man came clattering out, handcuffs and flashlight and holstered pistol rattling as he walked through a low, wooden gate. He was the same young officer who had given Bybee the parking ticket the other day. He was big—much bigger than he had appeared in the car—and his beard looked a bit fuller.

He clumped up to the two lawyers, looked at Watters, and smiled. "You on shore leave, Watters?"

"Sort of."

"What do you want?"

Watters stood up. "We want you to release Owen Parks. A jury just found him not guilty." He waved the manila folder. "It's all right here."

"That's funny."

"I think so." He pointed at Bybee. "This is Brig Bybee. He'll be working the case with me."

LeGrand looked Bybee over, staring, it seemed, at the way the clothes fit the lawyer so well, at the squared shoulders, the narrow hips. "I know. I'm LeGrand Little, deputy county sheriff." He did not offer his hand but kept them both hooked on his wide belt along with the other paraphernalia fastened there. "My dad's the sheriff. Lamar Little."

Bybee only nodded, but Watters slowly closed and opened one eye. "Sounds like a law firm, LeGrand: 'Little and Little.' " He pointed to the wall, to a framed photograph of the deputy standing with his father, enormously fat and a half-head taller than his son. "Maybe 'Little and Littler.' "

"Funny."

"Speaking of. Is ol' dad here?"

"He's out of town," LeGrand said. "Over to Hurricane." He pronounced the word "Hare-a-kin."

"That's too bad," Watters said. "Well, we need to get this road on the show. We came to see Parks. We only need about fifteen minutes." He nodded at Marla. "I called your girl this morning."

The deputy gave Watters and his odd uniform another look and then clanked back through the gate, letting it slap hard against Watters's knees. Like all good lawmen, LeGrand despised defense attorneys; they were godless men, his father had taught him, given over to chaos and the defeat of the system, always pushing, poking, filing writs, waving the Constitution in everyone's face, never obeying the law, really—the true law.

They walked down a short hallway, a cluttered office on either side, until they reached the jail proper. It was a plain-looking affair, cement floor and plaster walls, built years before simply to house shoplifters and drunks—Navajos, mostly, or jack-Mormons who couldn't navigate the grid. It was never intended for murderers, and LeGrand looked nervous as he stopped at a yellow-painted metal door and turned around.

"You got any weapons?" he said. "Or anything that could be used as a weapon?"

"Just fists of steel," Watters said.

"I'm not joking."

"None," Bybee said.

LeGrand roughly patted each of them down. "Go in," he said. He opened the metal door and stood aside. "I'll get Parks. You got fifteen minutes." The last words were almost lisped, as though something had slipped inside his mouth.

"Thanks," Bybee said.

They walked into a small room that contained nothing but a wooden table, the overvarnished, yellowish kind with thick, straight legs always found in schools, and four heavy wooden chairs. Watters slapped his folder down, sat, reached into his shirt pocket, and pulled out his pack of Marlboros. He stuck a cigarette into his mouth and slouched in his chair like a soldier in a bar.

"Look, Brig," Watters said. "I want you to get a feel for this guy. Talk to him like I'm not here."

Bybee nodded, the prospect of Watters's sudden absence heartening. He would, indeed, "get a feel for this guy," but it would be for the benefit of Watters, not himself. With tough questioning, he would demonstrate to this upstart how to work a client, how to push him into admitting guilt so that they could then, at last, deal with the reality of the crime, not some cockeyed conspiracy theory. It was one of the few things, a friend had once said, that he did with real spirit, with a sense of purpose.

After about a minute, the door opened again and LeGrand walked through, followed by a man dressed in blue jeans and a blue denim work shirt, faded stenciling over one pocket. He was of average height, thin, with dirty brown hair that hung well past his shoulders. A beard, a darker brown, billowed and curled around his face, so that his eyes seemed to be hidden, peeking out.

With one hand, LeGrand pointed Parks to an empty chair at the table, and with his other hand, pointed at the cigarette dangling from Watters's mouth.

"I know," Watters said. He plucked the cigarette away and dropped it back into his pocket. "Testing."

"Fifteen minutes," LeGrand said. He pointed to the door. "I'll be outside."

"Good," Watters said. "We'll be inside."

LeGrand left in a clattering of metal against the doorjamb, and Watters pointed at Bybee. "This is Brig Bybee," he said. "He's replacing Shields. He wants to talk to you."

With both hands, Parks reached up and parted his long hair at his forehead, smoothing it back behind his ears. Despite the strong smell of soap on him, he looked unclean, unwashed, something found huddled in a bus station or a free clinic. He waited, but Bybee, sitting tall and relaxed in the chair, said nothing and only stared at the man, stared through him. He had adopted, long ago, the psychologist's tactic of creating an awkward silence to draw his clients out, to make them reveal what was in their lurching, murderous minds.

"I am not guilty," Parks said.

Bybee made a face, arching his eyebrows in mock surprise. "State of Utah seems to think you are."

"I'm not."

"Well, tell me why you're not."

Parks's delicate fingers pushed back his hair again, and then he folded them on the table. The eleventh-hour substitution of one of his defense counsels did not seem to bother him at all; he accepted it as routine jailhouse procedure, like an unannounced change of bedding.

"I already told Ronnie everything," he said.

"So now tell *me*. I'm a newbie."

"I don't understand you."

"Look, Owen, the state says you took a gun and put it to the head of an old man and pulled the trigger. Do you understand *that*?"

"Yes."

"And for your trouble, the state wants to put you in a compound full of big, stupid queers so you can run a drill press the rest of your life. Do you understand *that*?"

Parks said nothing, and he let his head droop so that his hair covered his face and pooled on the table. He looked up, his eyes on the ceiling, shaking his head the way a woman would, clearing the hair from his face.

"You think I'm guilty, don't you?"

Bybee placed his hands on the table. "Owen, do you know why I—why we—were appointed to this case?"

Parks's adolescent voice seemed lost, drifting. "To get me off."

"No," Bybee said. "To make sure you get a fair lynching. The judge told me that in so many words."

"I don't understand you."

"How old are you, Owen?"

"Twenty. Well, almost twenty."

"You go to high school?" Bybee said.

"For a while."

"You ever been in trouble before?"

"You think I'm guilty," Parks said. "I'm not guilty."

Bybee took a deep breath. He was already tiring of this game, wrung out years ago by clients who wanted only one thing: to hustle their own attorneys. The trial, their defense, their eventual slide into a deep cesspool, were secondary to convincing only one person—not a judge, not a jury—of their innocence. The huckster's act and his mark were immediate, localized, narrowed to the jail cell. The shell game was on.

"I am not guilty, Mr. Bybee."

"Well, let's see, then," Bybee said. "Farnsworth was killed on Thanksgiving Day, about five o'clock in the afternoon. Were you out at his place that day?"

"Yes, but just in the morning. Mr. Farnsworth wasn't even there."

"Why were you out there?"

"To fix something in the barn. Mr. Farnsworth asked me."

"You go inside?"

"The barn?"

"No. The house."

Parks shook his head. "I never been in that house. Mr. Farnsworth never let me. Even if I wanted to use the bathroom." His face clouded in confusion, and he nervously tugged at his beard. "I told Ronnie all this."

"You ever have an argument with him?"

"With Ronnie?"

Bybee sighed and lowered his head, a piece of hair drooping downward. "With Farnsworth."

"No."

Bybee raised his head. "You ever yell at the old man?"

"No."

"Sure?"

Parks hesitated. "Yeah. Yes, sir."

Bybee leaned back in his chair. He could see the kid starting to waver, the veneer of schoolboy innocence beginning to crack.

"Some Indians say you were threatening the old man," Bybee said.

"They're lying."

"All of them?"

"Yes."

"You never went inside Farnsworth's house?"

"No."

"You never laid a hand on him?"

"No."

"You're as innocent as a baby?"

"Yes, sir. I am."

Bybee suddenly slammed his fist on the table, making both Parks and Watters jump. "Then why in God's name, you innocent bastard, did the police find a picture of the dead man in your trailer? Answer me that. In your own damn trailer!"

Parks's face suddenly changed; his eyes grew wide, then narrowed, and his whole body seemed to tense. He looked like a skinny mountain man dragged into the light by a howling mob, scared, helpless. Bybee waited; he had witnessed it a dozen times: the defiant, pathetic confession. The fraudulent web of conspiracy and shadows and ghosts in the night was about to come spinning apart. Parks was on the verge of blurting out the one, necessary, and nightmarish fact Bybee knew was the truth: he had blown another man's brains out.

"I didn't kill him," Parks said. His eyes filled with tears, and his mouth twisted downward. "I didn't!" He looked ten years younger, despite the beard, and he put one hand over his eyes and began to wipe the tears away.

"Besides—" He broke off and looked at Bybee, tormented, agonizing, and then at Watters.

"Take it easy, Owen," Watters said. He reached a hand over and grabbed the kid by the shoulder.

"What?" Bybee said. He leaned toward him. "Besides what?"

Parks raised his head and sniffed and calmed himself. "It's not a trailer; it's a camper."

"Oh, Lord *Jesus*!"

Bybee turned his face, and his jaw muscles tightened. Until this very moment, he had always heard the same sickness spewed out from these men's souls, had always seen the same ruined egos writhing before him, always wronged and misjudged—but always guilty. This was different.

"Brig?"

Outside, a truck blared its horn, but behind the thick walls, it was a thin cawing sound, like some winged monster circling and flapping overhead, the same sound he had heard in

Mackleprang's office. It screeched at him, and he knew then that this was his last case, Parks his last client. Bybee laughed to himself. It was a blurry, almost shameful end to it all—second chair to a brash oddball like Watters—but he was through; he knew he was through. His law practice was like the Kanab courthouse itself—aging, worn out, no longer functional, ruined by the Sipes debacle, the divorce, the decline, and now ready to be dismantled and replaced.

"Brig."

His last criminal case. The phrase had a calming effect, like the slug of Scotch that he used to enjoy. *The State of Utah v. Owen Parks.* He would have the final judgment framed or made wallet-size; he would show it, in his white-haired dotage, to his grandchildren, to visitors to his tidy, sterile room, to anyone, really, who would pretend an interest.

"Hey, studly. You with us?"

Bybee blinked at Watters, then took a deep breath, his chest swelling.

"Thought maybe we had lost you."

"No," Bybee said.

Parks had collected himself, and now he sat, his hands folded, staring at his two lawyers. Watters looked at his watch, then extracted a single piece of paper from his manila folder. It contained about half a page of typewritten text, single spaced.

"Before we go, Owen," Watters said. "I need you to sign this."

He slid the paper across to Bybee for his inspection. Bybee leaned forward and quickly scanned it, and then, alarmed, picked it up and read it, word for word. It was a detailed account, in the first person, of how, last Thanksgiving Day, Parks had argued with Farnsworth, retrieved a gun from his truck, and then made the old man drop to his knees and beg for his life. Then, the statement went on, he shot him point-blank in the head, took the man's picture, and drove happily away. At the bottom was a signature line, with "Owen Parks" typed under it.

Bybee gaped at Watters. "What are you doing?"

Watters snatched the paper from Bybee and gave it to Parks,

along with his cheap ballpoint pen. "Read this over, Owen," he said. "It's just a representation agreement. Says you understand Shields has withdrawn; that Bybee, here, is the new cocounsel, et cetera, et cetera. Standard stuff."

Parks took the paper and pen and carefully moved his eyes down each line, pausing here and there, until he looked up, nodding.

"Okay."

"You agree?" Watters said.

"Sure, Ronnie."

Watters pointed at the signature line. "Then just sign there."

While Bybee watched, every instinct telling him to rip the paper from Parks and tear it into pieces, the boy slowly scrawled his childish signature on the line.

"Good," Watters said. He took the paper and jammed it back into the folder and then looked Parks over, appraising the man's physique, mentally measuring him. "You know what size jacket you wear? Shirt?"

"No."

"Well, I'll guess. Just as well if it doesn't fit." He pointed at Parks's hair. "And I'm going to have a barber come in here and take off that hair and beard. In fact, give you a bad haircut."

Bybee waited for the reaction that always came, the explosion, the damnation, when these wretches were asked to cut their hair. Defense attorneys might as well ask their clients to lop off their cocks.

"Okay, Ronnie."

Watters grinned. "You know what a hayseed is, Owen?"

"No."

"Well, for this trial, you're going to become one. Right off the fucking turnip truck. Complete with bow tie."

"I don't understand you."

Watters didn't respond. He leaned his head back and blew a stream of air toward the ceiling, as though he were smoking. Some twisted scenario was obviously playing out in his head.

A hand rapped hard on the outside of the metal door, and almost instantly the deputy walked in.

"That's it," LeGrand said.

Bybee nodded and scraped his chair back and got to his feet. "That's for sure." He extended his hand to Parks, and the man took it with both of his own, clinging to him like a man dangling over a cliff.

"Do you think I'm guilty?" Parks said.

Bybee slowly withdrew his hand from Parks's grip. Five minutes ago, he would have given the man his standard reply, his speech about the irrelevance of actual guilt, the necessity of wrangling with the facts and evidence. But now, something was different.

"So long," Bybee said.

Watters waved his manila folder at Parks, and the two lawyers left the room and followed LeGrand back down the short hall and into the office. Marla Hamblin was still there, bent over a filing cabinet, and above her, on one wood-paneled wall, was a bulletin board, and next to it was a small campaign poster. It showed a picture of LeGrand, serious and clean-shaven, with LITTLE FOR SHERIFF printed beneath it.

Watters stopped and studied the poster for a moment, and then turned to LeGrand. "Maybe," he said, "it should be: 'Think big, vote Little.' "

"That's real funny," LeGrand said.

"I think so."

The deputy began to move toward the door, indicating they should do the same, but Watters stayed where he was. He bent toward the bulletin board and scanned the Polaroid photographs that were there: several of LeGrand, of Lamar, and an assortment of people, including Marla, and some children, all of them smiling into the camera.

"Your wife here, LeGrand?" Watters said.

"No."

Watters shrugged. "Guess they don't make wide-angle Polaroids."

In three furious strides, the deputy crossed the office and pushed Watters up against the file cabinet. The metal side popped, and Marla made a gasping sound and jumped to one side.

"You've got a wise-ass mouth, Watters," LeGrand said. His face was red, and one hand rested on the wooden baton clipped to his belt. "Somebody's going to close it for you someday."

Watters was the same size as LeGrand, perhaps bigger, and he put his hand on the deputy's chest and gently pushed him away. "Who? You?"

"Maybe," LeGrand said. He tried to take Watters by the arm, but the lawyer twisted away from him and marched across the office to the front door.

"C'mon, Brig. I think we're being thrown out."

While LeGrand stood in the middle of his office, hands on his hips, Bybee walked to the door and the two lawyers emerged back into the bright square of sunlight.

"That was real smart, Watters," Bybee said. He was angry and shaken, embarrassed by it all. "What's wrong with you?"

"Nothing." Watters calmly took the cigarette from his pocket and stuck it in his mouth so that it danced there. "I like to rattle cops' cages."

"Well, you sure as hell did that." Bybee shook his head and then pointed at the folder. "And this thing. You just got our client to sign a confession."

Watters laughed. "Hey, pretty slick, huh? That's the little test I was telling you about. See, I've been told that whatever it was that old man Farnsworth had out at that ranch, was a document. Maybe a diary or a will or an old deed—something." He took the sheet of paper from the folder and flapped it in the air. "Parks obviously can't read a goddamned word," he said. "So if he's illiterate, why would he kill to get a document that he couldn't understand? That has no value to him? That he wouldn't even recognize if it fell on his head? The answer is, that he wouldn't; but someone else would. I wanted you to see that."

"So this little show was all for my benefit?"

"Yeah." As it always seemed to do, his face suddenly changed, and he became serious, lowering his voice and shedding the clown persona, although it was difficult in the uniform. "I need to convince you, Brig, that this is not an ordinary, run-of-the-mill murder, and we can't defend it that way. Something very odd—odd as hell—is going on. I wish you would believe that."

"I do," Bybee said. He could not easily adjust to Watters's sudden mood shifts; he felt like a man in a car with a maniac at the wheel, swerving, skidding, then cruising slowly along. "*You're* odd." He pointed at the letter. "And you're stupid to be waving that around. State gets ahold of it, and—" He stopped; he wasn't clear about the evidentiary status of a homespun confession actually created by the defense.

"Don't worry, my friend," Watters said.

He withdrew a disposable lighter from his pants pocket, lit his cigarette, and then calmly touched the flame to one edge of the letter. In seconds, the entire sheet of paper was afire, and he dropped it to the ground, where they both watched it turn to ashes.

"All gone," Watters said.

"Lord."

Bybee had turned around, ready to leave, when out of the corner of his eye he caught movement at the front window of the sheriff's office. The old-style venetian blinds had been pulled up, and the bloated sheriff, Lamar, stood there, filling the entire frame. He watched them through the glass, his tiny eyes buried in the sagging flesh, and his hands were clamped onto his belt like pieces of equipment, the way his son's had been.

Watters saw him too, and he walked across the dried lawn and stood directly in front of the window, only three feet from the sheriff. The cigarette jutted out of the corner of his mouth.

"Hare-a-kin, my ass," he said, and then he came to attention, like a good sailor in his dress whites, and saluted.

As though it had been a magician's gesture, the fat man stepped back into the dark office and disappeared.

6

CARL Farnsworth had escaped years ago from the ranch —and his father's fervent Mormonism—by quietly packing a bag one night in the basement and, while the house slept, slipping outside, walking to the highway, and hitch-hiking to St. George. The next morning, he joined the air force and signed up for flight school.

Two and a half years later, he and his instructor pilot, flying cross-country, dropped below radar over the Kaibab and pointed the white T-38 straight up the gut of Johnson Canyon. They skimmed over the highway and the gullies of sage and thundered across the yard where his mother, Myrna, was washing out a pot, with the young Zolene playing nearby. The jet banked hard over the cliffs and circled back to Dishpan, taking aim on the old house again, and Myrna, with nothing to wave, took off her blouse and desperately flapped it as the trainer roared over her again.

He had finally returned; he had come screaming out of the sun, back to the canyons, back to his mother.

But the plane climbed almost straight up, away from the old woman and the little girl, away from the dying ranch and the red earth, and Carl rocketed into the hard sky over Hell's Bellows and disappeared.

"And that was that," Zolene said. She had been telling Bybee the story since they had turned off the highway and onto the dirt road. "He never came back; never visited. Didn't even go to his father's funeral." She looked out the window at the sprawl of old machines and weathered outbuildings. "He hates this place."

Bybee guided his Toyota past the gooey pond, parked near the house, and switched the engine off. The sun was low but hot, and in front of them, through the windshield, Dishpan shone as though it were a huge chunk of red glass, the light seeming to come from inside.

"That's too bad," he said. He leaned back in the seat, vaguely nagged by what Watters had told him about Farnsworth's will and the property, and Zolene's odd evasion of this fact. But he really didn't care; he was comfortable with it all, with her.

Over the past five days, they had been together constantly, meeting every morning at her aunt's house so that they could then go puttering around the area like tourists. They visited all the surrounding canyons and national parks, where they hiked and climbed—to the extent her leg would allow it—and several days before they had even made the three-hour drive to Las Vegas and fed quarters into slot machines all afternoon. And during it all, whether on narrow, sunny trails or in the bowels of a dark casino, they talked and laughed and teased each other, always drawing closer.

After each one of those delirious days, Bybee would rise the following morning in his tepee feeling—*knowing*—that she was changing him somehow, like an alchemist. He would stare at himself in the mirror, turning and touching his head as though he could detect visible signs of that change—tiny wrinkles smoothing, disappearing, the bit of gray hair around the ears darkening—Watters's body-snatcher theory in reverse.

There was no shape-shifting, of course, but for the first time in two years, the heavy, miserable cloak he had been lugging through his life was gone, discarded. He felt, finally, the way everyone always said he looked—sleek and quick, a toned athlete—alive once again and hopeful, the nightmare of Sipes and the divorce and his near disbarment mercifully dissolving.

"My relatives are just the opposite," Bybee said. "They just keep coming back and coming back."

Zolene laughed and reached into the backseat and retrieved a small bag of groceries that they had just bought at the IGA supermarket in town. They got out of the car and walked to the cement porch, and Bybee hopped up and then held his hand out and pulled her to his side. She was, as always, in blue jeans, but today, rather than a T-shirt, she wore a yellow sleeveless blouse. And, Bybee thought, unable to take his eyes from her, she was as stunning as ever.

"I don't know about this, Brig."

She had not been inside the house since her arrival in town a week before, and she was openly apprehensive. It had been violated before, its dark mysteries and tortured history inviting the trespassers, and she wanted it closed off, sealed forever. But she also wanted to share with Bybee the house and countryside where she had spent a good portion of her youth—happy and bright.

"It's up to you," he said.

She dug inside her blue jeans for the key, inserted it in the lock, and pushed open the door and walked in. They were in a tidy, low-ceilinged kitchen, the old appliances and wooden countertop scrubbed clean, still smelling faintly of soap. It was much different than the way Zolene had found it after the murder: pans and dishes and food scattered everywhere, even the refrigerator emptied, and the stove nearly disassembled.

"Well, let me give you the grand tour," she said.

She led him into the small dining room with its drop-leaf cherrywood table and old leather chair in one corner, and then into the bedroom, where a big four-poster stood, still gleaming with the oil she and her daughters had rubbed into it months before. She moved back into the dining room and stood before a closed door, the one leading to the basement. Bybee dutifully followed, his new blue jeans so stiff that they made a rasping sound as he walked, as though he were made of straw.

"That's where my grandfather was found," she said.

"I figured that," Bybee said.

Zolene ushered him into the living room, a large, cool, blue-walled place with a slanted cedar ceiling and, on three sides, big, paned windows framing the cliffs outside. Expensive antique furniture was arranged around a braided rug, and the wood floors were waxed and shiny.

"Wow," Bybee said. He stood in front of a flagstone fireplace, his head tilted back as he looked at the ceiling. "This is something."

Zolene watched him, pleased. He was standing where her grandfather had always positioned himself, a thumb invariably hooked into his jeans, a finger wagging. When she was a little girl, it was the same place he had stood while he and the others argued about what Doug had found, and her grandfather had shouted them down.

Bybee surveyed the rest of the room. On the stone mantel, beneath a portrait of a young boy holding a model sailboat—presumably Carl—lay a Polaroid photograph. He picked it up; it showed Zolene and her two daughters standing outside the ranch house, in winter, all of them bundled against the cold. Zolene did not offer to explain who took the photograph, and an uncomfortable spasm of jealousy gripped Bybee.

"I'll go make the sandwiches," Zolene said. "Then I'll take you up to the hills and show you my secret." She nodded at a plump, purple couch. "Take a load off."

Zolene limped from the room and Bybee, rather than sitting down, rasped across the room to inspect a bookshelf that was jammed and sagging with books, hundreds of them. Some were novels, others collections of poetry, but most were manuals and treatises on cattle raising and farming and irrigation. He began to turn away, but a partially shelved paperback caught his eye, and he recognized it from its streaky sky-blue color and the horn-blowing angel on the cover. It was the *Book of Mormon*, one of the older paperback editions, wedged halfway in between other LDS gospel.

He withdrew the book and slowly leafed through it, stopping at the familiar paintings of the muscled half-naked church heroes—Lehi and Alma and Mormon, of course. It had been several years since he had held the book, and he wondered now, as he often did before, if anyone truly believed what it said: that the American Indians once had sprawling cities, machines of iron and steel, gold coins and silk, elephants and chariots, books written in reformed Egyptian . . . and Jesus strolling among them.

He had started to reshelve the book when he saw two other books, along with magazines and separate, photocopied articles, stuffed behind the scripture, half hidden. He pulled out one book and looked at the garish red letters of its title—*The Mountain Meadows Massacre*—and then the other, smaller, in paperback, called *The Utah Massacre.* Both books bristled with scraps of paper that marked certain passages, and inside, when he turned to one such spot, the margins were filled with scrawled notes. Bybee scooped up the magazines and articles, perhaps a dozen or so, and quickly looked them over. They were written by a variety of researchers or scholars, the Tanners in Salt Lake, by Mormon historians whose names he vaguely recalled, and they all dealt with one subject: the Mountain Meadows Massacre.

He heard Zolene thumping unevenly back into the living room and hurriedly shoved the books and articles back in their place and turned around.

"Find anything interesting?" she said. She looked at the spot where the magazine pages jutted out, and one book was upside down.

Bybee turned back to the bookshelf and scanned some titles. "Oh, *Feeds and Feeding, Handbook of Water Control*—"

Zolene didn't laugh. "Actually, I used to read some of those." She held up a paper lunch sack. "Let's go."

They walked back through the kitchen, went outside, and set out toward the red bluffs, about half a mile east of the house. Bybee's hand found hers and drew her close to him, but Zolene seemed worried, preoccupied, and she said little as they plodded through the deep sand. Around them, the faint drone of flies was like a steady pulse of silence, a distant engine. Birds cawed, and now and then a rabbit would skitter through the sage in front of them and then vanish.

They labored upward, stopping only for Bybee to examine what he thought was an arrowhead or a shard of Indian pottery.

Finally, after struggling through a barrier of rocks and junipers, they reached the top of the bluff, a flat, windy area pushed up under a yellow ledge.

"This is the place," Zolene said. She set the lunch sack down on a large rock.

Bybee wagged his finger at her. "You mean, 'This is the *right* place,' Sister Swapp."

Again, Zolene did not laugh. She jammed her hands into her rear pockets and looked out over the area, the Hell's Bellows wind stronger now, whipping at her hair.

"So, where's your secret?" Bybee said.

Zolene pointed behind them, at a place where two boulders crowded together, and at the bottom, about two feet from the ground, a space widened into a dark hole about three feet in diameter. "I called this the Indian Cave when I was a kid," she said. "I hid arrowheads and pottery in there, things I found." She shrugged. "No big deal."

Bybee murmured something and moved close to her so that they stood, side by side. Below them, the land spread out for miles, the Kaibab Plateau and the Buckskin Mountains to the south and, looking north into the heart of the Grand Staircase, the whole of Johnson Canyon, red-walled and floored in alfalfa.

"This is the most beautiful place in the world," Zolene finally said.

Bybee stepped back and looked at her instead of the canyon. "I agree," he said.

She said nothing and, despite the ceaseless wind, the silence seemed to rear up again and engulf them, pull them apart. Over the past few days Bybee had grown accustomed to her moods—the occasional anger, the bouts of silence—and, as it had those times, now the fear seized him. It was the constant fear of losing her, the fear that she could now, any moment, just float off this ledge and drift away like a balloon, disappearing.

The strong wind had spread Bybee's black hair across his face, and he raked it back and dipped toward her. "What's wrong, Zolene?"

She did not face him. In the canyon, the wind rippled over

Wester Lewis's rich alfalfa fields, making them look fluid, like a wide, green river that flowed down through the cliffs until it reached her grandfather's ranch. There it faded into a plain of stubbled fields and died.

She turned and cocked her head so that the wind pushed her hair out of her face. "Brig, please don't tell Watters what you were looking at back at the house. Don't tell anyone, for that matter."

"I wasn't snooping."

"I know you weren't. I just don't want you saying anything to Watters. He—" She stopped and shook her head.

"He what?" The pang of jealousy, the panic, from a few minutes ago returned.

"I know we agreed not to talk about these things, the case, and all, but he hassles me; he calls me every day; he's even come by the house at night. He won't leave me alone. He asks me questions, over and over and over. He's driving me crazy." She looked apologetically at him. "He's even asked me for dates. He did the first time I ever met him."

Bybee slapped his hand against the side of his leg. "God damn!" He could picture Watters, his goofy shirt and the horsy grin, hovering over Zolene, pestering her, pawing at her. "Just tell him to go straight to hell!"

"I do, Brig. I have. It doesn't work. He thinks that I'm lying. He thinks that I know where Doug hid something."

"A document," Bybee said.

Zolene squinted at him, confused. "Yeah. How did you know?"

Quickly, Bybee told her of Watters's theory of the case, the rumor of the document, and the "test" he gave Parks in jail and of the man's stunning illiteracy.

"God," Zolene said. "He's such an . . . *asshole*! Sorry."

"Parks?"

"No. Watters—well, Parks, too. God, why does he try so hard to get that guy off the hook?"

"It's what he's—we're—supposed to do."

"Well, it sucks," she said.

Zolene walked over to the rock where she had deposited the

lunch sack and sat down, indicating that Bybee should do the same.

"Brig, that stuff you were reading back there. All of Doug's stuff?"

"About the Mountain Meadows Massacre?"

"Yeah. He was obsessed with it for years. For almost as long as I remember. He read everything he could about it. He was always mumbling about it. It ate him up. It ate him alive, especially the last few years."

"Why?"

Zolene looked at the sky. Two small puffs of clouds floated in the molten blue, strays that had wandered from a darker, larger herd that was gathering to the north.

"Doug got convinced years ago that the official version of what happened was wrong, a lie. I don't know why, or how, but he did. He was obsessed."

Bybee nodded. He knew that the "official version," as she called it, was only a footnote in the catechism, but something drilled into LDS heads, nonetheless. A Mormon pioneer and Indian trader, a man named John D. Lee, had organized a band of white men and Indians, and ambushed the Fancher wagon train. They murdered almost everyone and stole everything they could find. Lee tried to blame the church, and some believed him, but twenty years later, after being found guilty of masterminding the massacre, he was executed for it.

"I've heard that version," Bybee said.

"Anyway," Zolene said, "you know that old house?" she said. She pointed behind her without looking. "The one in the orchard? By where I found Max?"

Bybee looked over her shoulder down into the canyon. Part of the shingled roof of the dark old place could just be seen through the trees and vines. "Yeah," he said.

"It's called Lamb's house. Doug bought this place fifty years ago from a guy named Nephi Lamb. He lived in that house."

"Okay."

"Nephi—Neef, they called him—was the great-grandson of Josiah Lamb. You ever heard of him?"

"No."

"He was one of the guys at the massacre. Supposedly, he found something or was given something just before . . . it happened."

"Okay," Bybee said.

"Anyway, whatever Josiah Lamb ended up with was real important, some people thought. It was something that could hurt the church, cause all sorts of problems, maybe show that John Lee was right, after all. Maybe show that he was not guilty."

"And that's what all the rumors are about?"

"Yeah. That's why Lamb's house has always been a wreck. That's why they tore up Doug's house after he died."

"Who's 'they'?"

Zolene looked exhausted. "*He*, then. I don't know." She pointed north, up the canyon. "Back in the thirties, a guy named Freddy Crystal claimed he had found Montezuma's gold up there in the White Cliffs. Everyone in Kanab spent a month up there digging, going crazy. Then, when that was over, a bust, they found another fairy tale to go chasing after—Nephi Lamb and then my grandfather. Everyone thinks that he was hiding this secret document, whatever it is. The whole town's crazy, Brig."

Bybee exhaled heavily. This state would never change; it simply bubbled with secrets, frothed over with them, splashed in them. It derived its very existence from secrets—or the hint of them.

"But he wasn't hiding it," he said.

Zolene did not answer straightaway. In that frightening scene she had witnessed as a little girl, in the living room, moments after Doug had shouted at her father and Carl, he had stomped down into the basement. He emerged later with a leather pouch—dried and weathered—and had shaken it in the other men's faces.

"*The church can go to hell!*"

And she had watched from where she played on the rug, uncomprehending.

"No," she said.

Bybee touched her hand with his. "Zolene, I have never told Watters anything about us, about you, about what you tell me. Like you just said, we had a deal. He bugs me the way he bugs you. He hounds me. I can't get away from that, but I'm going to talk to him about leaving *you* alone."

She leaned over and kissed him on the cheek. "Thank you, Brig."

She drew back, and Bybee stared at her the way he did every day, the way she glowed in the bright sun, how her hair shone, and how her skin, a smooth, pure, waxy white, was almost translucent, as though you might see through the flesh—flesh he was aching to experience.

Over the past few days, there had been some intimacy, the hand-holding, the playful bumping, the teasing and nudging here and there, even a chaste, random kiss like the one he just received. He wanted so desperately to really kiss and touch her, to feel her mouth grinding against his, to slide his hand under her blouse, her bra, to cup her breasts, to gobble up that ghost-like purity the way he gobbled up everything else in his life.

But he was paralyzed, stricken by the numbing beauty of this woman, afraid to ruin the bond that he had so diligently and patiently forged over the last week. So he waited, gallant and abiding, taking the tantalizing slices of her that she offered up now and then, grateful just for that. He was out of practice, he knew, rusty from twenty-seven years of marriage and then, after the divorce, a series of weekend romps that could never rival this.

So, he knew, he had to find the right moment, the right mood, the right words. . . .

"I want to make love to you, Zolene."

Bybee watched her face for several moments to see how she would react, whether she would fling her arms open and gather him in, or jump up and scramble pell-mell back down the hill. But she did neither; instead, she leaned toward him and put her hand on the back of his head and held him while she pressed her mouth into his, her lips partly open, and then she let her hand brush across the back of his neck and down his arm.

"You really do?" she said, and she pointed at her left leg. "Even with . . . this?"

"Yes." He felt weak, watery. "There's only so many hikes we can take."

She laughed and looked into his dark eyes, at the angular, handsome face that she had found herself thinking about almost every waking moment for the last few days. He stood and gently tugged her to her feet and held her, kissing her and feeling her body press close to him. He tentatively brushed his hand over her buttocks, then pulled away and held her waist.

"We should," he said. "And soon." He lightly touched her breasts and then turned and looked at Farnsworth's house below, remembering the four-poster in the dark bedroom.

Zolene seemed to read his mind. "No, Brig." She kissed him again, briefly, and pulled away. "Not there."

"Then where? When?"

She turned her face only slightly, but the strong wind whipped her hair around her head, across her eyes. She reached out and took his hand and held it.

"Brig, you should know that I haven't . . . been with a man since Drew died. I've had some dates, a few friends, but I haven't really been able to . . . make love, you know. I mean . . . like you're supposed to. I'm scared, I guess." Again, she indicated her leg. "It's not real pretty."

"It doesn't matter to me, Zolene. It truly doesn't."

"I hope so. It's just that I need to find the right time, work up to it. Get my nerve up, I guess."

"Okay."

She leaned into him and kissed him again, a lighter, briefer kiss. "But it'll be soon. I promise."

"Soon," Bybee repeated. He could taste her mouth on his, moist and pure. "Soon."

The external world, Bybee thought, should have brightened at this point, like in the old movies, but the wind was suddenly growing cool, the sky darkening. To the north, over the Grand Staircase, the gray wall of clouds had risen, high and solid, almost like another tier of cliffs, and thin curtains of water were dipping earthward.

"We'd better go," Zolene said. She looked at the advancing black clouds and then snatched up the unopened lunch sack. "Things are going to get pretty ugly."

Watters sat in his car, on a side street a block away from Orma Frost's house, and listened to the rain pound on the roof, cold and furious. He had been waiting there, drunk, for over an hour, and his eyes hurt from staring at the street and house.

He lit a cigarette and then reached over, turned on the radio, and found a station, something faint and scratchy, a million miles away. Between his legs, he trapped a bottle of beer, like a big, glass cock, erect, and he grabbed it and took a drink. On the radio, the announcer suddenly switched from English to a toneless, chanting harangue in Navajo, and Watters reached out and angrily snapped the thing off.

"Fuck!"

In the gray curtain of rain, a car splashed past—a white Toyota—and Watters instinctively ducked, then sat up. The car stopped in front of the Frost house, and after a few seconds, Bybee jumped out of the driver's side, ran around the car, and opened the door for Zolene.

"What a gentleman," Watters said to the empty car. He spit and squinted harder at the house.

With his hand on her elbow, Bybee helped Zolene up the walk and they stood on the porch, talking. Then, as Watters watched, they kissed, briefly, and Bybee turned and sprinted back to his car through the rain. Zolene waved from the porch and disappeared inside the house, and Bybee turned his car around in the street and drove away.

"You dickless wimp," Watters said. He finished the bottle of beer and stubbed out his cigarette. "You waiting for an engraved invitation?"

He got out of his car and stood while the rain splatted

around him in big, loud drops. He crouched, and as though he were running through a tunnel, sprinted across the street and moved up the weedy sidewalk, jumping puddles. When he came to the Frost house, he stopped and squatted behind a low, wooden fence and wiped the water from his face. He looked around him; the street was dark and empty, and the only sound in the world was the roaring of the rain.

He slowly opened and closed one eye and stared at the house. The old lady was away at this time of day, and the back door was open. This, he knew; he had rehearsed this scene; he had actually executed a trial run two days before, trying the door and even walking inside the empty house.

His hand cupped his crotch, and he felt his cock thickening. He had wondered, from the first day he had seen her limp onto the porch at the ranch, what it would be like with a crippled bitch: maybe the one leg smooth and perfectly carved, locked around his back, while the other, a shriveled sack of bone and decayed muscle, slapped at his body like a tentacle. And he had dreamed something like that the other night, of her coming, screaming, as the withered leg slipped from the edge of the bed, dangled, and with a wet sucking sound, pulled away from the socket in a gush of black pus and blood and fell to the floor, still writhing, alive—

"Oh, fuck me!" he said.

In the backyard, he saw an Indian, a big, husky man with long hair, stooped in a flower bed, just under a window. At the same time, a light in that window came on, and Watters could see shadows and vague movements inside. The Indian straightened and pressed his face into the corner of the window, watching.

"Fucking Nav," Watters whispered.

Rain came off the roof in a cataract, and through it, he watched the Indian stare inside the room, half of his dark, oily face visible.

Suddenly Zolene's face appeared at the window, nose to nose with the Indian, separated only by the pane of glass. She opened her mouth, and even behind the window and in the roar of the storm, her scream was loud and shrill, like an alarm. The Indian ducked and almost fell backward, then ran back along the length of the house and turned the corner.

"Fuck!" Watters said.

He heard Zolene scream again, and he spun around and sprinted back down the sidewalk and across the street to his car.

7

ON the western end of town, where Center Street bends north and climbs up Long Valley through the Grand Staircase and into the old Mormon ghostlands of Deseret, a phony Indian village sits near the edge of Kanab Creek. Twelve stuccoed tepees—separate motel rooms with windows and air conditioners—form a ring around a campfire of cement logs. Plaster Indians, bleached white by the sun, their arms and ears and noses long ago broken off, stand around the fire like a tribe of mutilated ghosts, impaled on steel rods.

Overhead, a sign in the shape of an arrowhead grinds and creaks in a slow circle. It once read PIUTE VILLAGE, but a storm that had ripped down the canyon years before stripped away the *g* and the *e*, leaving it to read PIUTE VILLA, and it has remained that way ever since.

Inside tepee number nine, Bybee stood before a dresser mirror, the walls of the room tapering on all sides to a dark, cobwebbed point almost twenty feet above him. The cement floor had a few cheap Indian rugs thrown here and there, and the walls were decorated with plastic spears, artificial animal skins, and above the bed, a vinyl Indian headdress with bright pink feathers.

The frenzied call from Zolene had come five minutes before, instructing him to meet her on the highway, just north of town. She had babbled on the phone, half hysterical and incoherent, using language he had never heard from her, but he had finally gathered that an Indian had tried to break into her house, and that the sheriff was, predictably, nowhere to be found.

He had also gathered, or at least suspected, that she was drunk.

He hurriedly smoothed his shirt and combed his hair, and then left the room without locking it, got into his car, and drove out of the tepee village and back to Center Street. In a matter of seconds, he was out of town and driving north on the Long Valley highway, as Zolene had instructed.

The storm from an hour ago had passed, the rain had stopped, and now the nighttime air was cool and thick. He drove slowly, squinting ahead, not sure where she would be, and then saw the Mustang parked on the side of the road. The lights were on, the engine running, and Zolene's slender white arm was waving out the window.

He pulled up alongside the car. Zolene sat behind the wheel wearing a cowboy hat, and her shirt or blouse—or whatever it was—rode so low on her shoulders that it looked as if she was crouched there naked.

She leaned out the window. "Took you long enough," she yelled, and then she ducked back inside, put the car in gear, and drove away.

Bybee followed her as she drove deeper into the canyon and the red cliffs. There were few cars on the highway, and she drove recklessly, her hair beneath the hat occasionally blowing out her side window. She pushed the Mustang through the curves, along Kanab Creek where, in the crevices and half-caves under the cliffs, bales of hay stood piled, off-centered and tilting, like a child's blocks, and horses stood unmoving along the banks of the creek.

Finally, about a mile from town, her brake lights came on and she bumped off the road where the creek widened into a small lake. She pulled around a stand of tall willows onto a cement slab, turned the engine off, and waited until Bybee drove up beside her. They were under a cliff, hidden from the road, and parked on what looked like an old foundation to a building long since destroyed.

Bybee moved from his car to hers, and as he sat down, the unmistakable smell of alcohol swept over him. A half-empty bottle of Scotch lay on the console between them, and Zolene sat slouched against the door, the hat tilted down across her face. She was dressed only in a red nightshirt that extended midthigh, and it was decorated in front with the face of a blue wildcat. Her nipples were visible, poking against the thin cloth.

"You like Scotch and water?" she said. She took off the hat and tossed it in the rear seat. Her hair was tangled around her neck, and her eyes looked weak, rheumy.

"I used to," Bybee said.

"Well, there's the Scotch"—she pointed at the bottle and then out the window at the gloomy lake—"and there's the water."

"I wish you wouldn't, Zolene."

"Oh, don't give me that Boy Scout horseshit." She twisted in the seat, bringing her knees up, and put her naked feet on the seat. For an instant Bybee saw a thick ridge of skin, like a welt, darker than the rest, that twisted around her left leg, nearly running all the way to where the V of her panties showed. Zolene saw him staring and clamped her legs together as she reflexively dropped her hand to her scarred leg.

"Ah-ah," she said, and she wagged a finger at him.

"Why don't you let me drive you home?"

" 'Cause I don't wanna go home, that's why. 'Cause every time I turn around around here, there's some asshole Indian standing there grinning at me."

Bybee pointed at the bottle. "That won't help matters."

"It *does* help matters."

She turned and stretched behind her, pushing her breasts against the nightshirt, and then straightened, holding two paper cups decorated with animals and oversize letters.

"They're clean," she said. She saw Bybee staring at her breasts, and she looked down at them. "Those, too."

"Zolene—"

She raised her head and offered him a cup. "C'mon, Brig. The Word of Wisdom's not a freakin' law. You're acting like a bishop." She laughed, and then reached out and gently tapped him on the end of his nose. "I like that. Bishop Bybee. Has a nice sound."

He did not reach for the cup, and she dropped it in her lap. "Well, hell, bishop. You don't want to drink with me, then I'll have to find someone who will." She swung her legs to the floor, straightened in the seat, and started the engine.

The familiar rush of panic seized him, and he reached over and tried to turn off the ignition, but she batted his hand away. "Let's go to the sheriff's office," he said. "Make a report."

Zolene did not seem to hear. While the engine idled, she opened the bottle and began studiously pouring the Scotch into her cup, spilling some of it. She finished, capped the bottle, and then took a sip and looked at him.

"What kind of report? A book report?" She started to giggle, and then stopped. "Sheriff's an asshole, too. He won't do anything." She drank again from the cup and held it out to him. "C'mon, bish'."

Bybee looked through the windshield and studied the black surface of the lake only twenty yards away. In the moonlight, the water looked like a pool of oil, and the cool air was full of the smell of mud and rotted weeds—and the alcohol. He looked at the clear, odd-shaped bottle that lay on the console, the same bottle he used to crawl inside of every night, and after a while, every day.

Zolene pointed at the water. "It's called Three Lakes," she said.

"Looks like one to me," Bybee said.

"Yeah, it looks like one, but there's three—one on top of the other." She laughed. "Three layers, three lakes."

Bybee stared at her, wondering if she truly believed that nonsense. The top of her nightshirt had fallen farther down her shoulders and the bottom was creeping up her legs again, as though the whole thing were shrinking, contracting, dissolving off her body.

"In other words, it's bottomless," she said.

"Everything has a bottom," he said.

"Not this freaking lake," she said. If she was of a mind, she could tell him all the whispered stories about Three Lakes: murdered lovers and unwanted babies and chests of gold—even cars and trucks—forever tumbling downward in the black water, seeking a bottom that wasn't there. Instead she picked up the bottle and held it out to him, and when he refused, she put it down and placed her hand on the gearshift.

"I'm going to the Buckskin, bish'. It's been real."

She would go, he knew; she would order him out of the car and then squeal back out onto the highway and roar away from him—maybe for good. And he would be left standing there in the middle of nowhere in the middle of the night, in the middle of this free fall that was never going to end.

His black hair, carefully combed only minutes before, had crept down over his forehead, and he raked it back into place with his fingers and adjusted the glasses on his nose. Then he picked up the bottle. Just the feel of it—smooth and heavy and cool—was instantly reassuring, and he unscrewed the top. Zolene smiled, satisfied, turned off the engine, and gave him her cup and the one she had dropped.

"Attaboy," she said.

Bybee filled the bottom part of their cups with the Scotch and gave one back to her. He had been keeping count; it had been thirteen months, and now he touched his cup to hers, took a long, slow drink, and leaned back in the seat.

"Lord," he said, and he closed his eyes.

Zolene watched him, then balanced her cup on the dashboard and looked out over the steering wheel. Her head tilted to one side, and then the other, as though she were still racing down the road, leaning into curves. Finally, she slouched again against the door and swung her feet into Bybee's lap, wiggling her toes. Her nightshirt was high on her thighs now, her scarred leg and her panties clearly visible.

"Rub," she said. "Bishop. Bishop Bybee."

Already the liquor had warmed him, soothed him. He put his cup on the floor and shifted in his seat so that the heel of one of her feet dug directly into his crotch. He began massaging the inside of her feet, rubbing his thumb deep into the soft skin, moving the foot against his cock.

"So, tell me, Bishop Bybee," she said, "you believe him?"

"Believe who?"

"Watters. Your asshole of a friend." She took a long swallow of the liquor. "You think they got the wrong guy in jail?"

Bybee stopped his massaging and stared at her face, which in the thin light of the moon looked strained, almost streaked, her eyes bleary. This was not the way he had imagined, only hours before at the Indian Cave, that their lovemaking would begin.

"Watters is not my friend," Bybee said. "Besides, we promised we wouldn't talk about this."

"The hell with promises," she said. "You're not answering my question." She ground her heel harder against him, and he put his hand on her calf. "The question is: Do you think Parks is innocent?"

"It doesn't matter what I think; it only matters what a jury thinks."

"But I want to know what Bishop *Bybee* thinks."

He said nothing; his hand had moved slowly from her calf to the back of her right knee, like a spider.

"Well?"

"I think he's . . . different," Bybee said.

Zolene suddenly clamped her legs together, trapping his hand. She looked alarmed. "You think he's innocent?"

"Look, Zolene. I'll be honest." He pried her legs apart, and his hand resumed its climb upward, his knuckles gently brushing the thick scar tissue on her left leg. "I don't really care about Parks. An attorney should never care about his client; he should only care about the case. There's a big difference. If you start caring about the client, then you start believing him or her and all the wild stuff around you, and that's real dangerous. That's what Watters is doing, and it's dangerous."

"You don't make sense."

Bybee reached for the bottle and poured himself another big dollop of Scotch. She was right; his dramatic fall into his present limbo—into senselessness—had never been openly discussed between them, and he took a drink and looked out the side window. Through a gap in the canyon, he could see a faint rim of pale rock above the dark bluffs. It was the next tier in the Grand Staircase, the White Cliffs, a monstrous, quarter-mile-high wall that encircled the smaller red walls, corralling everyone, refusing to let anything—even the past—escape.

"Zolene, I've always been criticized all my life because I've never been very committed to anything that I do or try to do. I've always just done everything at half speed, without a lot of . . . conviction. I was a jack-Mormon, a jack-pilot in the Army, a jack-law student, even a jack-husband."

Zolene giggled. "A jackass?"

"Yeah, that, too. I never really took anything seriously—even a war—but I seemed to do all right, always landed on my feet. In my law practice, I've won my share of cases because I didn't really get too excited about things, about all the crazy crap that comes from clients. Instead, I just put together a good, solid defense based on the facts and the evidence. I worried about what a judge or jury might think, not what the client wanted to do or to prove." He looked out at the black water. "But I didn't do that with Becky Chu."

She smiled. "I do like that name."

"Bellard Sipes brutalized that little girl, Zolene. He . . . *fucked* her every which way you could imagine. Inside and out, upside down, back and front and sideways. He beat her; he degraded her; he used . . . things, instruments on her—" He stopped, the image of Sipes—his dead, gray eyes probably wild and bulging, his mouth open, as he bent to his work on the girl—too vivid before him. "That big, pompous man of God just reamed her out and ripped her up and left her hollow—dead. Spiritually dead. Then he lied about it."

"Asshole should be in prison," Zolene said.

"Damn right, he should."

The old anger was filling him up, molten and bubbling, and he saw that the cup he held in his hand was shaking. He placed it on his knee, steadying it, and put his other hand on her thigh again and squeezed it hard. She did not resist.

"I went charging into trial," Bybee said, "so pumped up about what had been done to her that I just . . . blew. I ranted and raved and screamed and took every cheap shot I could at Sipes. I tried to admit bad evidence—hell, I even *created* evidence. I berated witnesses; I coached witnesses; I threatened witnesses. I yelled about conspiracies and cover-ups and accused officers of the court—including the judge—of being Nazis. I violated every damned courtroom rule you could imagine. And all because, for one of the few times in my life, I got committed. I cared too much about my *client*, not the case."

"Brig . . ." Zolene's voice was weak, distant.

"I spent eleven months preparing that case, and thirty thousand dollars of my own money, me and my wife's money. The jury came back in twenty-eight minutes." He turned and looked out at the black lake and then back at her, his eyes as dark as the water. "Twenty-eight minutes. They took a leak, grabbed a doughnut, and returned a verdict."

Zolene tried to smile. "Well, it had to be done."

"Yeah, but not the way I did it. All hell broke loose after the trial. Church lawyers filed a grievance against me for my"—he raised both hands, one still clutching the cup, and clawed at the air with two fingers—" 'unethical behavior.' I had a hearing and a judge agreed and I was reprimanded. I was broke, and by then, my wife wouldn't even speak to me." He took his hand from her leg and pointed at the bottle that was almost empty now. "So I took up this, full-time. That was smart, huh?" As though apprehended, chastened on the spot, he dropped his empty cup on the floor. "A few months later I showed up at a murder trial, drunk on my ass, and the guy got convicted quicker'n shit. Another lawyer proved I was drunk, the guy got a new trial, and I got put on probation with the state bar."

"Jeez, Brig."

"Then I was shit-faced drunk one night and called Becky Chu and accused her of ruining my life. That was real smart, too. She filed a grievance, and—" He shrugged and turned to Zolene and opened his arms, displaying the simple, sad, unraveled life of Brigham B. Bybee, attorney at law. "Here I am."

"Here you are," Zolene repeated. She reached toward him and grabbed his hand and placed it again on her thigh, higher now, almost to her crotch.

"So, anyway," he said. His voice was slowing, slurring. "That's why I don't want to ever do that shit again. I did it one time—*one time*—and it bit me on the ass. Watters wants to do the same kind of crap now. Parks deserves a decent defense, and I'd like to give it to him, do it right, but Watters is—" He stopped; he had so much difficulty accepting and admitting this one, grating fact.

"In charge."

"Yeah," Bybee said, "but he shouldn't be. He thinks this town"—he waved his free hand over his head, pointing toward Kanab—"is full of—"

He broke off. She had now placed his hand on her panties and was rotating it in a small circle for him.

"Full of what?"

Bybee shifted his position and, without her help now, began massaging her, his long fingers feeling the hard mound under the panties.

"Hell, I don't know," he said. Her legs opened farther, and he could feel the dampness now, the warmth of her. "Evil scarecrows . . . something . . ."

Zolene laughed, softly, envisioning an army of creatures made of straw and sticks and old clothes marching across the alfalfa fields in the moonlight, sounding like Bybee in his new blue jeans.

"The Daughter of Zion," she said. Her voice, like Bybee's, was thick and slurred, and she closed her eyes. "Parks did it, Brig. Forget it. God, that feels good."

"Zolene—"

"It's time . . . now," she said.

She slouched farther into the seat and opened her legs as far as she could, coaxing his hand with hers. He clawed the panties to one side and slowly put his finger inside her. He stroked her, gently at first, feeling the wetness overtake her, then began pumping her with two fingers while his thumb probed higher. She squirmed in the seat, urging him even deeper, and she put one hand on the steering wheel, steadying herself.

"God, Brig!" she mumbled, and then swung her feet off his lap. She leaned toward him and fumbled at his belt and zipper.

"Show time," she said.

While Bybee watched, his arms out to his side, helpless, she yanked his pants open and with her long, white fingers, fought through his underwear. He was stiff, and she stroked several times and then released him, watching his penis remain upright above his rumpled clothes, something magic, swaying, slightly curved.

"Good," she said. She bent down and kissed the head of it, her red hair cascading everywhere. "Circumcised."

She suddenly sat up again and pulled the nightshirt over her head and threw it on the floor and faced him. The nipples on her breasts were large and hard, and Bybee leaned over, kissed one, and pulled back.

"Good," he said. "Uncircumcised."

He began to move toward her again, but she pulled away from him. Reaching back again, she retrieved the cowboy hat, jammed it on her head, and opened the door. She struggled out of the car and stood in the darkness in her panties and the hat, almost posing. She could very well have been a cowgirl model, something in a magazine, except for the ugly ridge of dead flesh that spiraled around her left leg like a red vine, a parasite.

She muttered something, then began to limp drunkenly across the cement slab, cursing as she stepped on rocks, until she stopped at the edge of the lake. She turned and faced the car, and then bent forward and stripped off her panties and stood, pointing at her dark wedge of pubic hair.

"This is the right place, Brigham." She turned and faced the lake. "I get it right this time?"

She waded waist deep into the black water—the upper half of her body floating for a moment like a marble, cowboy-hatted bust—and then splashed out into the water, keeping her head and hat above the surface.

Bybee carefully laid his glasses on the console, then scrambled out of the car and tore his shoes and socks off, then his pants and shirt, tossing them all in a heap inside the car. He slipped off his underwear and walked to the edge of the lake, hopping and mincing over the rocks as though he were walking on a hot bed of coals. He stood by her wadded panties, watched the highway, ready to crouch at the first hint of a headlight, and put his foot in the water. It was icy cold, but he took another step into the mud and reeds, his cock pointing at Zolene like a compass needle.

"C'mon, bish. Where's that Mormon pioneer spirit?"

He waded farther in, hissing at the sting of the freezing water, and then he dove in, and under, and came up splashing and windmilling his arms, gasping at the glacial impact of the water.

Zolene laughed at him and then swam easily, her head and hat still riding above the water, toward the cliff that formed one complete side to the small lake. She stopped at a jumble of large boulders that were half submerged and, even in the dim light, showed graffiti from decades of swimmers and midnight lovers. One word stood out among the others: FUCKS*.

"C'mon," she yelled.

Bybee dog-paddled frantically across the lake toward the rocks, trying to look smooth and practiced, and came up to her as she placed one hand high on the face of the boulder. Her breasts were just above the black surface of the water, and the nipples skimmed in and out of view.

Bybee clutched at a hole in the rock and then let himself sink, searching for a muddy floor. The water surged over his head, and he came back up spluttering, his hair pasted to his skull.

"Shit—"

"I told you," she said. "No bottom."

She held on to crevices in the rock with both hands now, and Bybee splashed behind her and grabbed her by her shoulders. The shock of the cold water had wilted him for a moment, but he was fully hard again and he ground against her buttocks, pushing at her. But his weight on her pulled them both away from the rock, and he went splashing back under as Zolene twisted away and swam toward a grottolike area.

She stopped and rose, and her white body eerily emerged from the water as though the lake had suddenly drained away. She stood waist deep near the shore, her breasts glowing at him. The cowboy hat was still on her head, cinched tight with a string and bead beneath her chin.

"C'mon, bishop."

Bybee struggled over to her and then, bouncing in the water, finally found the bottom—soft and slick and gummy—and marched toward her.

She pushed him toward shallower water, but Bybee grabbed her and threw her to the side, and she lay in the muck on her back, propped on her elbows, her left leg straight, unmoving, while the other was bent at the knee. Her head was out of the water, the hat still tethered to her, and the ends of her hair floated among the weeds and sticks and scum that drifted around her.

Bybee began to position himself, feeling for an instant the rope of dead flesh on her left thigh, but she violently shook her head and twisted to one side.

"No, Brig," she said, and she suddenly righted herself and pushed with both hands against his chest, forcing him onto his back, then moved alongside him and swung her right leg over his body.

"This way, bish'." She pointed at the cowboy hat on her head and laughed. "I'm dressed for it."

She bent forward, fumbling for an instant before inserting him into her, and then she straightened and slowly began moving, riding him, her breasts gently bouncing with every stroke. Bybee reached out with one hand to cage one, trying to finger her nipple, but she brushed his arm away and then leaned back, her long throat exposed, and began accelerating, feverishly pumping at him. For several minutes her body pounded against his, her eyes fixed, her wet hair whipping around her neck and shoulders, while Bybee simply gaped, helpless, moving instinctively, his head half-submerged in the dirty water, his face like a mask floating there, forgotten. Finally, her body seemed to tense, her eyes slowly closed, and she wriggled in tiny, frantic movements, grinding into him, forcing him deeper, more insistent, until her body began shuddering in electric waves. Her head snapped back, and she screamed—a short, piercing, primal sound of release that sliced into the canyon's silence and echoed forever against the dark cliffs.

She began to go limp, to fall atop of him, but Bybee thrust his hands out, grabbing her shoulders and straightening her. He pushed harder, reasserting himself, then moved slowly, tentatively, as though after her orgasm, they may have fallen out of rhythm, somehow, now clumsy and uncertain, like dancers moving to different music. But she easily melted into him as she had before, pressing backward and locking into him, their bodies now one again, moving together in perfect tandem, their wet flesh making loud, slapping, sucking sounds. He thrust harder and faster, breathing heavily, spit and lake water spewing from his mouth, moaning, muttering something as he watched her breasts quiver, the cowboy hat on her head bobbing in rhythm. He reached up and grabbed one breast, the move uncontested now, and he violently squeezed, then released it, and clutched her hips, the water foaming up around him in steady spurts each time he recklessly drove himself against her, into her.

"Zolene . . ."

He loosed a thunderous moan that had been bottled inside him for years and bowed his body, rising, still squirming, still emptying himself into her, as she finally fell toward him, her face into his, gasping, her hands, her forearms sunk into the mud on either side of his head.

They both remained still, waiting, without speaking, and then Zolene kissed him quickly and moved off his body and crouched there, on all fours, watching as Bybee lay in the shallow water, heaving. Her cowboy hat had not come off, but it was sopping, water dripping off it, half of it bent and crushed, and her neck and one side of her face were smeared with black clay and covered with leaves.

Bybee continued to breathe heavily for several moments, staring at the nighttime sky, at the welter of stars against the blackness. He was covered with mud and grass, a strand of stringy weed was wrapped around his scrotum, and he smelled like rotted food. He lay silent, unmoving, without speaking, breathing in gulps. Somewhere up the canyon, a cow bellowed and, farther away still, another answered.

When he caught his breath, he turned over and saw that Zolene had moved several feet away and was still on her hands and knees, her face just above the water, as if she were going to lap it up. He began to crawl toward her, but she suddenly gagged, her back arched, and she vomited into the black mud.

They rinsed in the lake and dried themselves off as well as they could, dressed, and then Bybee followed Zolene back to her aunt's house, the Kanab streets quiet and deserted as they crept through them. After he had made sure that she was safely inside the house, the door closed and locked, he drove back to the wretched Piute Villa.

Watters was waiting for him. He wore a blue-and-green Hawaiian shirt, and he sat in the middle of the plaster Indians, furiously drumming two plastic pens on his thigh. When he saw Bybee, he stood up and waved his hand.

Bybee parked his car next to his tepee and got out. He was still damp, and he smelled foul, like a lake creature. His hair was slicked back against his skull, flecked with tiny clumps of gunk, and he was still woozy from the liquor.

He walked up to Watters. "What do you do? Follow me around?"

"Sort of," Watters said. He sniffed and leaned toward Bybee. "Christ, Brig, you smell like shit. Booze, too. Where you been?"

Bybee did not answer. He looked angrily at the lifeless, crippled Indians that surrounded them, and then at a lone car crawling down Center Street.

"Look, my friend," Watters said, "we got a trial in four days. You realize that? You ready? You know the plan, Stan?"

"I know when the trial is, Watters."

"Good. I want you to do me a favor, then. I want you to ask

your little squeeze where she was last Thanksgiving Day. She won't talk to me anymore."

Bybee gaped at the man. "What in the hell are you saying?"

Watters dug a cigarette out of his pocket, lit it, and blew smoke out the side of his mouth, a street corner punk in a Hawaiian shirt. "Like I told you before, I'm checking things out. I got my investigator to fly down to Tucson a few days ago. On the Wednesday morning before Thanksgiving, your pal and mine, Zolene Swapp, left her kids with a friend in Tucson and took off. Boom. Disappeared. She didn't get back until late Thursday night. No one knows where she went." He kept the cigarette clamped between his front teeth and closed one eye. "Maybe she just went for a drive. Got lost. Something. Anyway, the old man that found Farnsworth, Wester Lewis, says he saw a white car at the Farnsworth place Thanksgiving afternoon."

Bybee swayed there as the smell of the lake muck rose up around him, dank and sour. He wasn't sure if he was hearing this right.

"You actually think she had something to do with all this?" Bybee said.

Watters shrugged. "Hell, who knows? I know that Carl Farnsworth was making a comeback. Was patching things up with the old man; was visiting the ranch now and then. Trying to worm his way back into the will, I guess."

"Who told you all this shit?"

"It's not shit, my friend. It's in pleadings filed right here in good ol' Kane County." He pointed east, down the street, toward the courthouse. "Carl contested the will, the one that gave your girlfriend everything. He says Swapp was interfering with his relationship with his father, had used undue influence, et cetera, et cetera. Swapp's fighting it." He pulled on the cigarette. "Lying about it, too. You know that."

"No, I don't know that, Watters. Why don't you go straight to hell?"

Watters grinned. "I will, someday. Probably see your girlfriend there. Fact, guess I'll see a lot of lying little cunts there."

Bybee took a step toward the man and balled his right hand.

He had not thrown a punch at another man since he had been in the Army, at Fort Rucker, thirty years ago, but he was ready to slam a fist into the vile, arrogant mouth in front of him.

"Go ahead," Watters said. His face had hardened, and he squared himself, showing his wide shoulders, the muscled arms. "I'll rip your nuts off."

Behind Watters, a woman, the night clerk, appeared at the door of the office tepee, watching them, and Bybee stepped back. His hands were shaking again, and he folded them under his armpits for a second, then let them hang, useless.

"That deputy was right," Bybee said, his voice lower now. "Someone's going to close that mouth of yours someday. For good."

Watters laughed, and his face changed, almost contorting. "Gee, who will it be? You? The big war hero?"

"Stay away from her," Bybee said.

"Oh, I forgot. She's all yours."

"That's right."

Watters sniffed theatrically and wrinkled his nose. "Well, you'll never get any pussy smelling like a fucking sewer."

For an instant, like a locker-room braggart, Bybee considered telling Watters where he had just been, just done.

He turned away and walked back to his tepee and opened the door. He had left the air conditioner on, and now a cold wall of air swept over him, chilling him.

"One more thing, Brig," Watters yelled. "Guy around here swears he saw a red-haired woman in a white car driving through town last Thanksgiving. Thought it looked like Swapp. Just for your information."

Bybee walked into his tepee and closed the door.

Watters turned to an armless Indian standing a few feet away, one that had a big blackened hole gouged into its plaster crotch.

"Later, my friend," he said.

8

NOT too long after V-J Day, a group of Kanab men, most of them the same Watermelon Indians who had chased the flyers into Milt's Tavern years earlier, erected a wooden sign at the south end of town, near the Arizona state line. It was a large, hand-painted thing, viciously sledge-hammered into the ground, that read NO JAPS, but after the first hard rain, it read NO JARS, and it remained that way for years.

Now, of course, that sign is gone. But near the same spot, about a hundred yards away, is a spread of trailers and campers and tents, all connected together by a sagging webwork of orange and black electrical cords. It is known officially as a "trailer park," but it is truly a refugee camp, a place where the drunks and drifters of Kanab are collected and sorted out . . . and watched.

Watters drove under the wooden sign—RED LAND ROOST—to the rear of the lot, and parked next to a group of metal drums that overflowed with garbage. A few yards away, outside a gray, humped trailer, three Indians sat in folding chairs and watched him as he got out of his car.

"Afternoon," Watters yelled.

He waved a notepad and walked across the weedy lot until he stood in front of the men. One, obviously the oldest, a man in a new denim jacket, had a leathery face and long, gray hair that hung to his shoulders. The other two were younger, probably in their early twenties, and were dressed in dirty, long-sleeved shirts and blue jeans. And one was thickly built, his face an oily, blackish brown with a missing front tooth—the same man Watters had seen crouching outside Zolene's window last night.

"Afternoon," Watters said again.

The three Indians said nothing; they sat around a blackened fire pit drinking beer from quart bottles, and several empties were scattered around their feet. Behind them, in the pinkish light of late day, the western tail of the Vermilion Cliffs—darker and smaller than the others—trailed off toward the polygamist lands of the Arizona Strip and faded into black clouds.

"My name's Ronnie," Watters said. "I'm a lawyer who represents Owen Parks."

The Indians all stared at him, and one, the smaller of the younger two, raised the beer bottle to his mouth, drank, and then leaned forward. Watters bent, expecting to shake hands, but the man only broke wind and sank back into his low chair, silent and unmoving.

"We know," the older man finally said. He had gray eyes, the color of his hair, and he pointed at an aluminum lawn chair folded against the side of the trailer.

"Thanks," Watters said.

He walked to the trailer and unfolded the chair, and then set it down facing the other three. He rested the notepad on his lap, almost like a tray, and placed his big, red hands on top of it. None of the Indians spoke, and Watters looked at the cliffs, at the black clouds brewing there.

"Looks like rain again," Watters said. " 'Bout had enough of that shit." He looked at the man with the missing tooth, the prowler. "Haven't you?"

The man said nothing, and the older one, after drinking from the bottle, held it out to Watters.

Watters hesitated, unsure about drinking after these filthy guys, then took the bottle. "Yeah," he said. "I could go for that." It was still cold and sweating, and he took a deep pull of the beer, puffed out his cheeks and belched, and gave it back. "Thanks. Nice and cold."

The prowler laughed and pushed his long hair back from his face. "*Nice and cold*," he mimicked, his voice high and nasal.

Watters's face changed, hardened, and he stared at the man for several moments, sizing him up. "That's what I said, Cochise."

The prowler tried to meet Watters's fierce stare, but he was drunk, his eyes red and weak, and he finally shrugged and picked up the beer bottle. "Fuck," he said, and then he muttered something to the older man in Navajo. His voice was deep and slurred, like a mumble from a cavern, a lost race.

"His name's Charlie Fall," the older man said. "Not Cochise." He pointed at the other young Indian. "That's Donald Burton. My name is Jerome Hatathlie. People call me Old Jay."

"Whatever," Watters said. He had backed them down, quelled an uprising. "People call me Ronnie. So call me Ronnie."

"What do you want here?" Old Jay said.

Watters flipped back several pages of his notepad and extracted two pieces of paper, each filled with typewritten text, with scrawled signatures at the bottom. He read the names silently and smiled.

"I want to talk about these." He waved the documents. "They're copies of statements that these two guys, here, gave to the police." He looked at the prowler, Charlie Fall, who swayed, slit-eyed and drunk, in his chair, about to live up to his last name.

"What about them?" Old Jay said. His voice was steady, deep, with no accent.

"Well," Watters said, handing the photocopied documents to the younger men, "are these your signatures?"

Before either of the Indians could react, Old Jay grabbed the papers and looked them over, then showed them to the other men. While he waited, Watters eased back into his chair and held his hands up, palms outward, spreading his fingers, as though he were counting them: *One little, two little . . .*

Old Jay handed the documents back to Watters. "Yeah. They signed them."

"And they're true and correct?"

Old Jay looked at the other two and shrugged. "Yeah."

"Well, let me read one of them. Hell, they're almost identical."

For the next minute, while the three Indians solemnly watched and listened, Watters read Fall's statement that he had given to the police. It detailed his expected testimony: that he had often been in "close proximity" to Parks and heard him talk of "eradicating" Farnsworth because the old man was "Satanic." The statement went on to claim that he believed Parks to be the "perpetrator" because he had seen him once with a pistol, and that on Thanksgiving Day, Parks left early in the day and did not return until that evening.

During Watters's reading of the statement, Old Jay sat, calmly sipping his beer, but he looked concerned, and at times he openly frowned and mumbled to himself.

"All right," Watters said when he finished reading. He turned to Fall. "I'm going to give you a little test, a quiz. I like quizzes. Ready? What do the words *proximity, eradicate, Satanic,* and *perpetrator* mean?"

The young Indian looked at Old Jay, and the two exchanged quick, harsh words in Navajo before Old Jay turned back to Watters.

"He doesn't like tricks," Old Jay said.

"It's not a trick, my friend," Watters said. He reached into his shirt pocket and pulled out a cigarette and plastic lighter and lit up. "He has no idea what these words mean, does he?"

The other two men huddled and talked again, and then Old Jay raised his head. "He doesn't understand you," he said, and he stared at the ground, worried.

"All right." Watters squinted through the cigarette smoke at the statement, and then looked at Fall. "What kind of pistol did Parks have? Revolver? Automatic? Glue gun? Ray gun?"

Again the Indians spoke hurriedly to one another, and Old Jay barked something at him, then shook his head. "Automatic."

"Thought so," Watters said, and he let out his breath. The police report clearly concluded that Farnsworth was shot with a revolver. "I don't suppose any of you has ever seen Parks with a camera?"

"No," Old Jay said.

"Okay." Watters pretended to study the statement, and then looked at Fall. "When is Thanksgiving Day? October? November? I forget."

The Indian glared at Watters and then finished the beer in his bottle and leaned back in his chair, smiling.

"Right," Watters said. He folded the statement, slipped them between the pages of his notepad, and then looked at Old Jay. It was apparent that the man was distressed by what Watters had just done, and by the answers that the younger Indians had given. "We need to talk, my friend," Watters said. He grinned at the other two and then returned to Old Jay. "Just you and me."

The old man understood, and he nodded and growled something in Navajo to the others. For several moments they argued in a language long buried in these cliffs and canyons, the unwritten language of the spirits, the World War II code talkers. Finally the two younger men struggled to their feet, and after standing and studying Watters for several seconds, they walked across the lot and disappeared inside a battered trailer.

When they were inside, Watters dragged his chair closer to Old Jay, and the dust rose around them like red smoke. Behind the Indian, along the line of dark cliffs that disappeared into the horizon, the wispy wall of black was stalled, hovering.

"Why are they lying?" Watters said.

Old Jay pointed a dark finger at a spot about twenty yards away, where the burned-out shell of a trailer sat blackened and skeletal, like a rotted carcass.

"Because they do that."

"Who does that?" Watters said.

"The police. Sheriff Little."

"They burn you out? Run you out?"

"Yeah."

"If you don't cooperate? If you don't do what they say?"

Old Jay picked up his bottle, drank from it, and then shrugged. "Yeah."

Watters studied the trailer's remains for a moment and then turned back around and wrote something on his pad. About two dozen sheets of the notepaper had been filled over the past few days with his cramped scrawl, and they were all bent back, curled around the cardboard backing, creased and wilted.

"You here last Thanksgiving?" Watters said.

"Yeah."

"All day?"

"Yeah."

"Who was with you?"

Old Jay looked sad, worn beyond his years, and he looked out at the highway, east, along the line of Vermilion Cliffs that were still in the sun, those near Hell's Bellows.

"Them other two," Old Jay said, nodding toward the younger Indians' trailer. He then looked back out at the cliffs, trying, it seemed, to see beyond them. "And Owen Parks," he said.

"All day?"

"Yeah. All day."

Watters slowly folded the wrinkled pages over and tapped the notepad with his fingers. He hadn't realized it, but his heart was pounding in his chest, throbbing. "You testify to that in court?"

"No. They'll burn me out, too."

Watters shook his head. "Maybe not, my friend."

Old Jay picked up his beer and drank deep, watching Watters as he did. He seemed to believe the white man.

"You ever heard of the Daughter of Zion?" Watters said.

"No."

"It's a secret white posse. They use Nav—Indians to do their dirty work." He pointed at the trailer where the other Indians had entered. "I caught one of those guys, the big one, Fall, hanging around a white woman's house last night. Farnsworth's granddaughter. You know why?"

Old Jay stared at the ground. "They probably ask him to. The sheriff. I don't know."

If he could have, Watters would have jumped to his feet and pumped his fist in the air and hollered, but the nylon webbing in the chair was so old and loose that it had formed a pocket, and he remained trapped like a fish in a net.

For the next several minutes, he talked to Old Jay, gaining his confidence and asking him details about the sheriff and his deputy. And Old Jay told him how the officers routinely patrolled the Red Land Roost, swaggering through the lot like prison guards, and threatened and intimidated everyone that lived there—especially the Navajos. When he was finished, Watters had convinced the man that he and the others should testify—truthfully—about everything that had gone on here, and certainly last Thanksgiving Day and the perjured statements.

Watters put his pen down and pointed at the huddle of metal houses around them. "Which one of these trailers is Parks's?"

Old Jay shook his head. "No."

"Oh, c'mon," Watters said. "He lived—"

"Not a trailer," the old man said. "It's a camper."

Watters hooted. "Oh, Christ! Does it really matter?"

"Yeah," Old Jay said. He pointed a dark finger—almost black—at a field of dirt and rocks and weeds about two hundred feet south. "All the campers are down there."

Watters finally struggled out of the sunken chair and stood up. Old Jay was right; he had not noticed when he drove in that the northern half of the big lot—the half in which he stood—was filled only with trailers. The other half was used only for trucks and their campers.

"Which camper?" Watters said.

Old Jay pointed his finger again, this time directly at a squarish camper on aluminum stilts, with small windows and a tiny door. Next to it was parked a battered pickup truck, cream colored with patches of dark primer, like a pinto horse.

"Is it locked?" Watters said.

The old man nodded. "Yeah. Sheriff did it. Sealed up."

Watters tucked the notepad under his arm and thrust his hand out at Old Jay. The men, both outcasts of a sort, had formed an instant alliance, a bond.

"Thanks, my friend," Watters said. "For a hell of a lot more than you know. I'll be in touch about you testifying at trial." He was already formulating how he would word the place of service on the subpoena: *Red Land Roost, silver trailer, third from the end*... "And don't worry about the sheriff anymore." He knew, if he could invoke the protection of the court, the Indians would be safe, shielded.

Old Jay stood up and shook the other man's hand, then pointed again at the southern half of the lot. The air had the smell of rain now, a heavy odor of wet earth and junipers and sage, and of something else, something dank.

"Take a real close look when you go down there," Old Jay said. He smiled, finally. "Look around you good. Real good. Look for signs."

"I will," Watters said. He was already walking away, and he waved his hand. "Later."

The road to the southern part of the lot was rutted and, in places, washed out by yesterday's rains. Quickly Watters picked his way around the red, mushy puddles and the miniature ravines, and eventually found himself in the middle of a rough semicircle of campers, some attached to trucks, others standing alone. As the old Indian had said, the narrow door to Parks's camper was crisscrossed with bright yellow tape, and a square of paper glued there warned the reader that the Kane County Sheriff's Department had quarantined the thing.

For a few moments Watters walked around, looking for anyone he could question, puzzling over Old Jay's advice to "look around you good." But the place was deserted, it seemed, with nothing out of the ordinary, and so he turned to go back. But as he walked up the road, he noticed that a chain-link fence marked the eastern boundary of the lot, and wired to it, about waist high, was a metal sign, rusted and bent, barely visible. He walked to the sign, squatted down, and after brushing away the mud on it, squinted at the faded lettering. It took him several seconds to absorb what he read.

"Ho-ly . . . *shit*!" he said.

He stood up and began running up the road, back toward the trailers and his car.

"Goddamn!" he yelled, but he laughed as he did, and he raised his fist to the sky, almost as a tribute to the startling intervention from above—or from Old Jay.

The rain did not come, but a cold wind did, and it blew through the lot, fierce and strong. Old Jay stood under a wooden canopy attached to his trailer, but in the cloudy half-light that had arisen, he looked blurred, like a spirit, an ancient shaman that had shimmered into existence and pointed the way.

Watters shouted at him. "Thank you!" He saluted, a sloppy flick of his hand over his eyes. "I get it."

The wind whipped around him as he sprinted to his car and jumped inside, his whole body shaking. He found a clean page on his notepad and began furiously writing, muttering as he did.

When he was finished, he looked back at the trailer, but the Indian was gone. He started his car and drove quickly out of the Red Land Roost, his tires splashing through the day-old puddles of pink water, and turned back toward town.

Watters arrived at the courthouse just as Thurma, the court clerk, was leaving, but he coaxed her back to her office and, explaining what he needed, waited, nervous and pacing, until she returned. She had found exactly what he wanted, and he paid her six dollars, gave her a kiss on her cheek, then raced up to the second floor.

Mackleprang's office was closed, the lights out, so he clattered back down and ran back to his car. The wind was still blowing, although not as hard, and he drove the two blocks to the Red Hills Motel on Center Street. He parked and ran under the motel's overhang to a blue-painted door with the brass numerals "109" tacked near the top. He had been there twice in the last few weeks—all on business, which this visit certainly was.

He pounded on the door and leaned back. "Judge!" he yelled. He waited, his ear turned toward the room. Inside, he heard voices—one deep and hushed, maybe a television or radio—and then there was silence.

"Judge Mackleprang!" he yelled again, and he reached over and frantically tapped on the window.

After a moment, he heard the rattling of the security chain, the bolt lock thrown, and the door slowly opened, exposing a sliver of light. Mackleprang pressed his pink face to the opening and frowned. He was not wearing glasses, and his eyes seemed lost and unfocused. Behind him, Watters could hear the soft murmur of the television set, and he smelled smoke—cigarette smoke.

"What do you want, Watters?" Mackleprang said. He opened the door a bit wider, showing his white shirt and narrow tie, the same damned ugly tie that the man wore as religiously as his garments.

"I need to talk!" Watters said. Despite the fact that he had driven here from the courthouse, he panted, out of breath, as though he had run the entire distance. "It's important."

"What do you want?" the judge said again.

"I need a continuance. About a week, that's all. Just a week."

"Why?"

"I just . . . found some things. Discovered things. I need my investigator down here. Maybe an expert, too." He stopped; he knew he had to give the state thirty days' notice of any expected expert testimony, but he shook his head, as though to erase the rule. "I need an investigation."

"Wol, of what?" The judge opened the door a bit wider; he looked worried, his eyes focused on the sky over Watters's shoulder.

"Of the deputy, the sheriff. Everything. This shit called the Daughter of Zion, the Red Land Roost. Witnesses have been threatened. The search of Parks's camper—"

Mackleprang pushed his soft hand in the narrow opening, palm outward. "Watters, every defendant always makes crazy claims."

"Parks is not making these claims, goddammit! I am."

The judge angrily shook his head. "Wol, it doesn't matter anyway. And you don't have to cuss. I'm sorry, but the trial goes on as scheduled."

"Judge, I can blow this case wide open. I can. The state's witnesses are lying, and I can prove it. The evidence is bad. It's a bad search. But I need time, a week; just a—"

"We'll pick a jury Monday."

The judge began to close the door, but Watters suddenly slammed his fist against it so hard that it violently swung wide open, the edge of it hitting the judge's chin. Before Mackleprang could recover, Watters stomped in, but he stopped when he saw another person sitting on the bed, beginning to stand. A cigarette burned in an ashtray on the bedside table, next to the *Book of Mormon*.

"Well, I'll be a son of a bitch," Watters said. "Look who's here."

Mackleprang's chin was bleeding now, and he grabbed Watters by the arm and tried to push him back toward the door, but he wrenched his arm away. When the judge grabbed for him again, his hand glanced off Watters's shoulder and he jammed his fingers into the larger man's face, just below the eye.

Watters's reaction was swift and instinctive, his fist coming in an overhead, swinging arc, like a blazing throw from a softball pitcher, striking Mackleprang squarely in the groin. The judge grunted like an animal and instantly doubled over, dropped to one knee, and then toppled to the carpeted floor. He lay there, spittle bubbling from his mouth, and cupped his crotch like a child.

Watters began to move toward the other person in the room, who was standing now, paralyzed with it all, but then quickly walked back outside and closed the door. His breath came in loud gasps as he stared into the fist-sized hole he had made a minute earlier in the painted wood.

"I don't *fucking* believe this."

9

THE war bonnet on Bybee's head smelled of sweat and hair spray, and the stiff feathers scratched his face, but he kept it on and crouched behind the wheel of the covered wagon. In front of him, Zolene sat on the porch of the house and worked at an empty butter churn, while a small boy sat beside her. She would not look up, and behind her, two terrified faces stared out of the windows.

"Now!" someone yelled.

Bybee and another Indian rose, and he rushed directly toward Zolene, whooping, waving his tomahawk in the air.

"No!" Zolene screamed. She threw her hands up and shielded her face. "Please!"

Bybee leaped on the porch and reached for her, knocking the shawl to the floorboards as his forearm grazed her breasts and then tightened around her neck. Next to him, an Indian in blue shorts and a Hawaiian shirt was clubbing the young boy by a flour barrel. Zolene screamed again, and Bybee hauled her to her feet and waved the tomahawk at her head.

"A white woman!" he yelled.

Behind him, out in the dirt yard, he could hear the pleas for help and the shrieking blood yelps. A man stood alone atop a gallows, a noose around him, his neck bent, his tongue dangling out of his mouth.

Someone laughed and took the man's picture.

Bybee pushed Zolene through the open door of the house, past the frightened faces painted on cloth and the two-by-four struts and sheets of plywood.

"You're crazy," she said.

"You heap-um pretty."

He moved to kiss her, but the feathers from his war bonnet brushed against his mouth and made him draw back, spitting air, and she ducked away.

"Cut!" a man yelled. He was big and overweight, with a bristling beard, and dressed entirely in a black cowboy outfit. "That's a wrap."

From the lot outside, applause and laughter erupted, and Bybee turned away from Zolene and looked through the door of the phony house. Dell Glazier, the man in black and the owner of the Pow-Wow, waved a megaphone in front of him as a pudgy tourist in shorts and a golf shirt stopped turning a crank on a fake camera. About two dozen other tourists stood behind him, cheering, as their friends stripped off their costumes.

"And that's how it was done," Glazier yelled. He had a gun belt strapped under a bulging paunch. "The movies in Kanab."

Bybee pulled off his war bonnet and tossed it along with the rubber tomahawk into a cardboard box that a young boy was tending, and then took Zolene by the arm and moved her away from the crowd. They strolled hand in hand over to the gallows, and after paying the cowboy there, mounted the wooden stairs. Zolene slipped the noose over his head and they both posed and made faces, and the cowboy took their picture with a Polaroid camera and gave them the print.

After a few minutes, the tourists were herded into the dining room, leaving Bybee and Zolene alone in the middle of the phony town. He held her in front of him, his hands on her waist, and smiled at her.

"You look nice," he said.

Zolene looked at his baggy khaki pants and oversize shirt he had bought that morning at Duke's, still creased and wrinkled. "You, too," she said.

He squinted at her for a moment, unsure if she was making

fun of him—but he didn't care. He had arisen this morning and, at first, bounded around his tepee like a high school kid with his first, panting crush—buoyant and dizzy, even singing. He was convinced, as he had stood in the cone-shaped shower, soap dripping from him, that he was in love with her, truly and unmistakably in love, and that he must, like some gallant in a Victorian novel, declare himself. But as the shower's spray ran cool, the freakish reality of last night sank in: Watters's visit and his dark, disturbing, ominous theories.

She was distraught, he reasoned to himself, troubled over her grandfather's secretive life and violent end, and that accounted for her lying—if, indeed, she was. But he also had no valid reason to doubt Watters and what his relentless probing was beginning to uncover, other than that he truly disliked the man.

So an hour later, as he had hunched over his coffee and the *Salt Lake Tribune* at the Trail's End, he had decided that he must ask her, that he must dispel this uneasy speculation once and for all, and he had spent the rest of the day agonizing over just how he would broach it.

"Want to eat?" he said.

"Yeah," Zolene said, and she pressed against him. "Sure do."

Inside, the tourists were already in line, inching past steam cabinets where two men and two women in cowboy outfits filled up trays with meat and beans and bread. Bybee and Zolene joined them and, their trays finally heaped high, found a table in one corner and ate while the tour bus revelry eddied around them in a murmur of talking and clinking silverware.

They conversed, like everyone else, but in low voices, husky with their new intimacy, and at times Bybee reached for her hand and stroked her white fingers for a few seconds before she glanced around and put her hands in her lap. They talked of inconsequential things—the staged shoot-out, the food, even the weather—as Bybee deliberately steered away from last night's soggy romp. There would be other times—drier, more intimate, traditional times—and he would wait. Besides, the image of her smeared in muck and vomiting like an animal was still too vivid, too much to relive at the moment.

When everyone had finished eating, cowboy-hatted waitresses began clearing the trays from the table, and Glazier walked to the front of the room and clicked on a microphone. After introducing Donell Bunting, the cook, to roaring applause, he told of the history of Utah, of Kanab. He explained the struggle of the Mormon pioneers against the Indians, the elements, and even the federal government, which had sent troops, a century before, marching against the Saints' polygamist shadow government in the fledgling—and failed—Republic of Deseret.

Glazier droned on, and about the time he finished, LeGrand Little appeared at the doorway across the dining hall and surveyed the place. As always, he was in full regalia, the gray uniform with all its dangling equipment, and when he saw Bybee and Zolene, he walked over to them.

"Hello, Mr. Bybee," he said. His beard seemed almost fully grown now, a thick, brownish blond. He nodded at Zolene. "Miss Swapp."

"Hello," Bybee said. He looked back at the wide doorway and saw the sheriff standing outside, waiting, a big uniformed blob on the sidewalk, rocking to and fro like a buoy.

"I'm looking for Watters," LeGrand said. He hooked his hands in his belt and, as though he might discover the man crouching among the tourists, looked over the dining hall.

Bybee jerked his thumb over his shoulder toward Parry Lodge. "Across the street in the Barry Sullivan Room." He winked at Zolene. "Whoever he was."

"He's not thar," LeGrand said. "Hasn't been all day. Car's thar, though."

"What's wrong?" Bybee said. "He illegally parked?"

Lamar looked down at him. "That's funny. No, your friend slugged Reed Mackleprang over to the Red Hills Motel, hurt him bad; damaged some property. I think we ought to talk to him, wouldn't you say?"

Bybee looked at Zolene and then at the fat sheriff standing outside. Despite Watters's arrogant recklessness, he could not imagine that the oaf was so stupid that he would assault a judge, especially a soft, timid man like Reed Mackleprang.

"I suppose," Bybee said. He was still having difficulty picturing Watters striking Mackleprang. "And he's not my friend."

"No one's friend, looks like," LeGrand said. He looked at Zolene—or rather, at her breasts—and then turned and walked back to the door.

Bybee watched the deputy retreat and disappear, and then fell silent. He was trying to decide if Mackleprang, off duty in a motel room, would still be considered an officer of the court, and if so, how serious an assault on him could be. Even if it was a misdemeanor, as it probably was, it would still land Watters in a criminal court and, more than likely, when the state bar was through with him, without a law license.

"Lord God," Bybee said.

Zolene pushed her hair from her face. "I knew something was wrong with that guy."

Bybee slowly nodded, agreeing, then snorted out loud; he and Watters were not friends, as he had assured the deputy—everyone—but they were now brethren, of sorts, two wretches that had authorities hovering over them. Maybe *that* was the shrieking, flapping thing that he kept hearing.

"Let's go," Bybee said.

Zolene got to her feet, and Bybee walked around the table and stood by her, waiting. Across the room, Glazier and two others were emptying water from the steam cabinets, and when he saw them, he took off his black, ten-gallon hat and swept it above his head in a broad arc, like a matinee hero.

They walked across the dining room and through the front door and stood on the sidewalk next to the wooden Indian. The sun was down, now, and the cool evening air had already settled over the town. Across the street, cars and pickups ringed the church, and scores of locals were gathered on the grass next to the building. On a lighted stage, several people were skipping back and forth, flinging their arms out and yelling at the crowd.

"What's going on over there?" Bybee said.

"That's called the Gazebo," she said. "A play, some music and dancing. They do it every week in the summer."

"Well, let's go see it."

He theatrically cocked his arm and bowed, and Zolene laughed and placed her hand inside his elbow, and he grandly led her toward the church.

When they reached the Gazebo, he guided her among the men and women that were standing on the dance floor and watching the performance on the stage. Several children, blindfolded and dressed in white smocks, crouched atop stepladders and called out to some adult actors below, who stood and held their arms open, smiling. The children shrieked and moaned and extended their hands, beseeching the ones below to receive them, to relieve them of their sightless torment, and to take them down.

"Spirit babies," Zolene whispered to him.

Bybee smiled, his dark eyes softening, peering into her. "I know. Even jack-Mormons have seen that before."

They found an empty bench at the far end of the dance floor and sat down. After a few minutes, when the play ended, a three-piece country and western band took the stage, and a clogging troupe of five young girls in fringed skirts and vests, cowboy hats, and clattering black shoes began dancing.

They watched the cloggers, or "country tappers," as Zolene kept calling them, enjoying the Kanab night, the feel of each other—but both preoccupied with the disturbing news from LeGrand. Finally the cloggers finished, one of the band members exhorted the audience to dance, and couples began to shuffle out to the floor.

"Jeez," Zolene said. "Things will never change. Look at this."

The couples on the dance floor looked as though they were at a nostalgia party. The women were all middle-aged matrons with unpainted faces and colorless clothes and home perms, and the men looked their counterparts: slacks, laced leather shoes, short-sleeved shirts, short hair—and the new beards, of course. They were all throwbacks, all good creatures trapped within the high red walls of these cliffs, born in this sere Martian landscape and raised on the milk of Mormonism.

And now they were grown-up spirit babies, believing desperately in events of centuries ago and trusting those who told them it was all true if their resolve was true, if their testimony was strong, if they believed in the restoration of all things, and above all, if they believed in their prophets.

Across the dance floor, Bybee saw DeWitt Hightower, the prosecutor, walking toward them, weaving in and out of the dancers, his head down and cocked, determined. He was dressed in new blue jeans and a western shirt, and he came up to them and made a short, comical bow, bending as though to display the top of his partially bald head. Like Mackleprang, Hightower had come to Kanab early, days before the trial, and had stayed on, Bybee guessed, maybe to absorb the local color or, more realistically, to escape the bureaucracy back home.

"Evening," Hightower said. His eyes looked smaller than Bybee remembered, and he puffed out his cheeks as he looked at Zolene. He didn't bother to introduce himself to her, and instead turned to Bybee.

"Guess you know that your hotshot cocounsel beat the living daylights out of Judge Mackleprang."

"That's what I hear," Bybee said.

"God, where'd they get that guy?"

"Same place they got you, I suppose: a law school. We're all cut from the same bolt of cloth, DeWitt."

"Bullcrap," Hightower said, and he instantly looked at Zolene, embarrassed. "Sorry."

Zolene put her fingers in her ears, pursed her lips into a moue, and fluttered her eyelids. Bybee laughed, and Hightower turned toward him.

"Guess it's just you and me at trial."

As he and Zolene had walked over here, Bybee had been mulling over that prospect: Watters arrested, booked, and jailed, and then Bybee left alone to give Parks a decent defense—finally. But Watters could always bond out, Bybee knew, and maybe be ready for trial.

"I guess," Bybee said.

"I don't like this, but I've been . . . told to try and plead this thing out. So I'm offering to drop this thing to manslaughter."

Bybee did little to disguise his surprise. The government, he knew, had never made an offer to settle the case; now they were trying to strike a deal that may have Parks only spending . . . what? Half as many years in prison? One-fourth? He strained to remember the sentencing guidelines, the confusing matrix of years and offenses and criminal history that entangled a defendant's life. Bybee looked at the prosecutor; he had done this long enough to know that there had arisen a sudden weakness, a softening.

"You said you were told to offer this," Bybee said. "Who told you?"

Hightower hesitated, and then looked apologetically at Zolene and shook his head. "Mackleprang." He held up his hand when he saw Bybee gape at him. "He just *suggested* it. The courts don't dictate state policy."

Bybee knew he should guffaw in Hightower's round, red face. For whatever reason, Judge Mackleprang had just ordered—not suggested—that this case be settled . . . and on the heels of being physically assaulted by a defense lawyer. Something had gone awry in the prosecution's camp—or with the court—but whatever it was, he knew that the opening gambit of reducing the charge could be improved upon further, maybe even a recommendation from the state for probation. He was, by default, the de facto first chair now. He felt comfortable, at the controls in a familiar command position, and he instinctively reacted to seize the upper hand and work a respectable plea bargain for his client.

"Sorry," Bybee said. "No deal."

"All right," Hightower said. He seemed relieved. "That's good. Judge wanted me to offer; I offered. It stays on the table for twenty-four hours, then it's back to murder." He puffed his cheeks out, then exhaled. "Had my way, we'd hang the guy."

He bowed again at Zolene and stomped off across the dance floor. The two of them sat in the vacuum of his departure, and for several minutes, they silently watched the dancers scrape and skate across the cement that had been sprinkled with corn meal. Bybee was dizzied by it all: Watters's bizarre theories, his attack on the judge, and now the desperate, unexpected plea bargaining. Something was not right, and he looked at Zolene, who seemed just as bothered. He had to ask her now; he had to eliminate at least one of these mysteries.

He stood up and pointed across the park. "Let's go over there. Quieter."

He took her by the arm and guided her off the floor and walked slowly across the grass to a picnic table about a hundred feet away. The air was becoming cooler, so they sat huddled together on one side of the redwood table and watched the dancing from a distance. The rest of the park was dark, but the dance floor and the white-painted Gazebo burned bright and floated on the grass like a moored ship, waiting.

"Nice," Zolene said.

Bybee twisted and kissed her, finally, and they held each other for several moments.

"Did it bother you?" he said. He pointed back to the dance floor. "That talk about Parks?"

"Yes. You guys trade in souls the way ranchers around here trade in hay and horses. Yeah, it bothered me, even if it was about Parks."

Bybee nervously smoothed his pants. "You're still convinced Parks murdered your grandfather?"

She pulled back from him, her eyes wide, her mouth open, like the painted faces back at the frontier town. "Of course, Brig. Aren't you?"

Bybee realized that she had been too drunk last night to remember their conversation. "Well, I told you before, I don't know." He felt his right hand shaking, and he put it firmly on his thigh, steadying it. "But Watters thinks he didn't. In fact, he's pretty sure he didn't."

Zolene made a hollow, breathy laugh. "Jeez, that Daughter of Zion crap."

"Maybe." Bybee hunched forward now, his forearms on his legs. "Look, it may not matter now. Watters might be out of the picture, but he's been suspicious; he suspects . . . lots of people."

"That's crazy."

Bybee looked out over the park, at the Gazebo glowing in the darkness. A woman there laughed, and her voice seemed to float through the air, never dissipating, never falling.

"Zolene, when was the last time you saw him?"

"Watters? Jeez, I don't—"

"No," Bybee said. "Your grandfather. Did you see him on Thanksgiving Day?"

She did not say anything, but only stood up and turned her back to him and stared at the lights of the Gazebo.

"Look, I'm sorry," he said.

With a quick shake of her head, she limped several feet away and held her arms with her hands, hunched against the cool air.

"Zolene?"

He walked over to her and put his hand on her shoulder and tried to turn her around, but she pulled against his hand and remained closed off to him. He stepped around her and looked into her face; she was crying, and two tears had run down her white face, leaving almost identical, glistening trails on her skin.

"Oh, Lord," he said. "I'm sorry."

He put his hand to her face to wipe away the tears, but she blocked it with her own. Her eyes were half-closed, her mouth trembling, and in the thin light she looked wild or deranged —angry.

"Is that how you guys do it?" she said. "The good cop–bad cop thing? You come at me both ways? Watters hounds me and harasses me, and then you take me on hikes and buy me dinner and . . . then make love to me."

"Zolene—"

"Is that how it's done, Brig? Is that how you lawyers get a confession out of people? Is that how you win? Is that how you get your fucking clients off?"

A burning had spread down his head and neck, and he moved to face her again. "No, Zolene. That's not what I do. It's just that Watters is—was—eaten up with this. If he's still on this case, then I want him off my back—your back. We can settle this, straighten him out."

He reached out to hold her, to bring her closer, but she violently twisted away and limped several more steps toward the Gazebo and away from him, away from everything they had created over the last week, every smile, every kiss . . . last night.

"Jesus, Brig."

"Zolene, I've never really thought that you had anything to do with all this."

"Right." She turned around. "I don't want to see you anymore, Brig. I mean it. I knew that first day that I should never let all this happen. You're all alike, and I'm sick of it—fucking *sick* of it!"

It washed over him now, again: the breathless panic, the desperation, the fever that was now burning through his brain, blinding him. She was shrinking right before his eyes, disappearing, and there was nothing he could do.

He looked over her shoulder at the Gazebo. It *was* a ship, now, its horns blaring, calling everyone to board, passengers already lining the rails and laughing, beckoning the Saints to come and sail into the darkness, calling to Zolene.

He was dizzy, and he felt as though he were going to be sick. "I've got something else—"

He took her arm with one hand to try and guide her back to the bench, but she jerked her arm away.

"Leave me alone. I'm going home."

From the Gazebo, the music drifted across the grass, and a breeze flowing down from the canyon, from a world beyond the red cliffs, stirred around them. Two of the cloggers walked close by them, their shoes clattering like a train on a trestle, and behind them two lovers walked with their arms around each other.

"I love you, Zolene."

She suddenly began crying again, violently shaking her head back and forth as if some demon had entered her, possessed her, and then she tilted her face to the sky.

"Oh, *God!*"

From across the park, the music stopped and the master of ceremonies announced that the dancing was over, the night ended.

"Zolene, don't let all of this go. I meant what I said; I love you."

He stood apelike in front of her, his arms dangling, waiting for her to stammer out some timid declaration of her own, maybe, something that would bring her back, would salvage what they had.

"God damn you!" she said.

She turned and limped across the grass, and at the same time someone began turning off the lights around the Gazebo, one by one. She moved farther away from him, and as each light was snapped off, part of her disappeared, by degrees, until, in the one light remaining, all he could see of her was the dim glow of her hair.

Bybee spun around and saw a man standing next to the circuit box on the stage, ready to flip the last switch. Bybee desperately waved his arm in the air.

"Wait."

The last light was turned off, and the entire park went black.

10

RONNIE Watters's only brush with formal Mormon instruction came as a child in Ogden, when he was coaxed by an LDS chum into attending an after-school class called "Primary." There, after some readings from the *Book of Mormon* and the *Doctrines and Covenants*, a man in a short-sleeved white shirt and heavy-rimmed glasses stood behind two cardboard boxes, one marked GOOD and the other BAD.

One by one, the man held up a packaged food product and beamed as the roomful of kids (with the exception of Watters, of course) squealed "Good!" to the can of corn, and the carton of milk, and the loaf of bread, or "Bad!" to the package of cigarettes, the can of coffee, the Coke.

And the man dropped each, reassuringly, into the appropriate box, smug with the righteousness of the day's lesson that said the world is easily divisible into distinct halves: corn versus coffee, good versus evil . . . bright truth versus a shadowy version of it.

Watters sat on the dirty mattress in Old Jay's trailer at the Red Land Roost and sorted and divided his research in the same way the Primary instructor had urged. On one half of the filthy bed, he piled useless sheets of yellow legal pad paper, pages and pages of his scribbled notes that had been scratched through and *X*'d out, rejected, thousands of words that meant nothing, led nowhere. But on the other half he carefully set out the notes that had been copied over or underlined, emphatically circled, a small pile of pages that he numbered in the upper right-hand corner and clipped together.

When he had finished, he took the smaller pile and read them through, then read them again. Had he been back at the Barry Sullivan Room, where his laptop and small portable printer sat, he would have typed everything up, printed it out, and even saved it on a diskette.

But he wasn't there; he could not even go near there. After he left Judge Mackleprang sprawled on the motel room floor, clutching his balls and bleeding, he knew that the sheriff or his deputy would be combing the town for him within minutes. So he had driven his car immediately back to his own motel, then, with nothing but the clothes he wore, quickly walked the mile or so out of town to the Red Land Roost, ducking into the weeds at the side of the road every time he saw a car approach. And when he finally appeared at Old Jay's trailer, at the only real hiding place he could think of, the only friend he could think of, the Indian had invited him in and offered him a quart of beer and a bed.

Now, a day later, he sat with his pile of notes and lay back against the thin-paneled wall and closed his eyes. He was tired, exhausted; he had barely slept last night, and he had spent nearly the entire day running to the telephone booth near the trailer park's shabby, tin-roofed office, calling his investigator in Ogden. And he had tried Bybee at the Piute Villa a dozen times, but the man never answered.

The trailer reeked of kerosene and wood smoke, and the Indians in the trailer next to Old Jay had begun howling and hollering, drunk, and were playing loud music. He rolled over on his side and looked out a dirty window at the setting sun.

"Fuck it," he said.

He got to his feet, folded the smaller pile of notes into a thick square and stuffed it into his back pocket, then threw the others into a cardboard box full of empty beer bottles. Old Jay was gone; he had left an hour before, promising to bring back food, a new supply of cold beer, and some news about Bybee, but Watters could not wait.

He left the trailer and hurried across the rocky lot to the phone booth, groped for change in his pockets, and dialed the number of the Piute Villa. He waited, but as it had done all day, the phone in Bybee's tepee rang endlessly until the clerk cut in and disconnected the call.

"Shit," Watters said.

He dug a cigarette from his pocket, lit it, then leaned against the glass, smoking, trying to clear his head. To be sure, Bybee was not at his motel, nor was he at Orma Frost's house; he had called there several times, and each time he was assured, once by Zolene herself, that they didn't know where he was—or even care.

He pulled at his cigarette, puzzled, and then realized where the man was, the only place he could be. The last time he had seen Bybee, he reeked of sludge or manure—something—but there was also the unmistakable odor of alcohol about him. And there was only one place in this godforsaken Martian hellhole where you could get liquor, real liquor, something other than beer: the Buckskin Tavern.

He had begun to leave the booth when he heard the sound of an engine, and he turned around, expecting to find Old Jay bouncing over the potholes in his truck, maybe even Bybee sitting next to him. Instead, he saw the sheriff's car, the roof-mounted lights blinking crazily, crawling through the Red Land Roost. LeGrand was driving, his head swiveling back and forth, and as usual, his whale of a father was lolling in the backseat, his head barely visible.

Watters instinctively ducked and squatted on the floor, masked from LeGrand's view by an opaque, plastic pane that surrounded the bottom half of the telephone booth. Peeking just above, he watched LeGrand pilot the car to the back of the lot, by Old Jay's trailer, then stop and back up, reposition it, and stop, the engine and lights off.

"Shit," Watters said again.

He looked past the car, to the south, at the same rutted path he had taken yesterday to the lower half of the lot, where he could still see Parks's camper perched next to a collapsed wooden fence. Beyond that, he knew, as he had seen when he was tramping around there, was a dense stretch of the scrub pine and juniper that was everywhere—the "pygmy forest," as the locals called it, a place no cars or trucks could go. On the other side of that barrier was the Buckskin Tavern.

He looked back at the sheriff's car, then to the wooden fence again, trying to estimate how many seconds it would take for him to sprint there, and the reaction time of LeGrand.

He waited, watching, and when one of the Indians in the next trailer came thumping out the door, laughing, both LeGrand and his father turned to watch them.

Quickly Watters opened the door to the phone booth and sprinted across the lot, only fifty feet in front of the sheriff's car, and then headed down the slope to where the campers sat. LeGrand was more sluggish than he thought; Watters was halfway to the end of the lot when he heard the car door slam and the deputy yell at him. He twisted around and saw that LeGrand had begun to give chase, then stopped and stood in the middle of the lot, his weapon still holstered.

In a matter of seconds, Watters had leaped the rotting fence and was out of the Red Land Roost and into the pygmy forest. It was almost dark, but he could still see, and he ran south, through the trees and the sage, following a gully, then a cattle trail, and finally he came up on a broad, cleared area—the parking lot of the Buckskin Tavern. It was filled with cars and pickups, most of them with "Ski Utah!" license plates, and one he instantly recognized: Brig Bybee's white Toyota.

He got up and hurriedly crunched over the gravel lot toward the building. Despite its reputation as the longest bar in Arizona, the place looked ordinary and unimposing: rock and brick walls and a sloping tin roof that, except for the glowing beer signs in every window, could very well have been a warehouse. Through the tin overhang in the front, square holes had been cut to allow Lombardy poplars—Mormon trees, as some called them—to shoot upward, and a metal cowboy made entirely of old auto parts stood in front, surveying the parking lot with lug-bolt eyes.

Watters stood by the metal man for a moment, looking back up the highway, north toward Kanab, and then opened the door and walked inside.

The bar was undeniably long, extending from one end of the building to the other, and despite the low-slung lights over some pool tables and the dozens of neon beer signs hanging everywhere, the place was dim and cold-looking and smelled of pine disinfectant.

Bybee was the first person he saw; he was the only person at the bar. The rest were at the pool tables, or stuffed into the cheap vinyl seats that lined one wall. In the mirror over the bar Bybee saw him, and he swiveled on his stool just as Watters came up to him.

"Well, lookit this," Bybee said. He was obviously drunk, and he raised a half-empty glass to him. "Man on the run. I thought your ass would be in jail by now."

Watters shook his head and quickly sat down. His face was glistening with sweat, his hair matted, and he still smelled like Old Jay's trailer.

"He grabbed me—took a poke at me." He looked around him at all the cowboys in their jeans and boots, most wearing ball caps rather than the straw Stetsons that were in season. "I need to talk to you."

Bybee's eyes were red and watery. "Oh, yeah? What do you wanna tell me? How to fuck up a relationship? How to try a whiz-bang case?"

"I'm serious, Brig. LeGrand's on my ass, and I need your help."

"Well, you can go fuck yourself, Watters. The last time I tried to help you, I got shit on." He smiled and then threw a mock punch at Watters's face, making him flinch. "You *asshole*!" he yelled.

At that moment the bartender came up and watched Bybee for a moment. He was a skinny cowboy with a welt on his neck and a wad of dirty gauze and tape wrapped around his left wrist.

"Problem here?"

Bybee waved his hand in small circles, as if he were washing a window. "No problem, man. Just talkin' over old times with my buddy."

The bartender turned to Watters to confirm what Bybee had just said, and Watters nodded, ordered a beer, and the man left.

"Listen to me, Brig," Watters said. "There's been some—"

"I don't wanna listen to you. I've listened too much to you."

Watters took one of the tiny cocktail napkins stacked on the bar and wiped his face. "Well, maybe this will make you listen. Do you know who I found sitting in Mackleprang's room yesterday? Who's down here making sure this case goes the way he wants it to go?"

"The tooth fairy. The Easter bunny. Shit, I don't know."

"Bellard Sipes."

Bybee stopped and tried to focus on the other man. Across the room, the jukebox started up, and a scratchy country and western song came warbling out of speakers at either end of the bar.

"Sipes?" Bybee said.

"You're damned right! Your old pal, the next president and prophet."

Bybee opened his eyes wide and held them open, and then exhaled. He tried to picture Sipes—squat and bullet-headed, the boiled-looking eyeballs, a thug in a dark suit—sitting in a motel room in a forgotten little Mormon cow town.

"Why?"

"I'll tell you why," Watters said. He stopped and waited as the bartender set his bottle of beer down and retreated. "I spent all fucking day on the phone. Sipes is the man in charge of dealing in documents in the church. He buys all the anti-Mormon shit people find in their attics—old affidavits and letters and legal documents—anything that can hurt the church." He took a deep swallow of the beer and belched. "And they pay big bucks."

"The church?" Bybee said. He was having difficulty following Watters's rapid, frantic speech.

"Damned right. And I told you that whatever Farnsworth had on that ranch was a document. And I'll tell you something else I found out, my friend. Old man Farnsworth went to fucking Salt Lake two days before he died!"

Bybee grinned. "The city, not the lake."

"It's not funny, Brig. My investigator found the motel he was staying at. Look, Farnsworth was broke; he was going under; banks were calling in some notes. He needed cash, and he knew how to get it—a lot of it. I think he took that document on his ranch, whatever the hell it was, up to the church and tried to sell it. But he couldn't strike a deal. Sipes probably told him to stick it up his ass. But Sipes *knew*, then, what Farnsworth had."

Bybee shook his head, the alcohol and loud music thrumming through him now, disorienting him. "What about your . . . scarecrows? The bad asses, the Daughter of—"

"Brig, I told you two weeks ago that this Daughter of Zion was muscle for the church. It exists, but it doesn't. It's not the Lions Club, for Christ's sake. It's just some toughs who are going to help the church, anywhere. Around here, it's that fat-ass sheriff and his son. Sipes calls them up, tells them what the old man has, and they probably send a fucking Nav out to whack him and tear the place apart. Then they set up Parks, plant this bullshit evidence in his camper—"

"No, no," Bybee said, and he grinned. "His trailer."

"No, Brig. It's a *camper,* and that's damned fucking important. Look, I've been holed up at the Red Land Roost, with a Nav named Old Jay. He knows what's going on. The sheriff fucked up—bad—and if you'd listen—"

Watters suddenly broke off as he saw the glow of headlights from the parking lot sweep across the curtained windows and then fade. He waited, and then the door opened and a stringy cowboy and his heavy-assed girlfriend walked in and disappeared into the rear.

Bybee finished the last of his drink and raised it in the air, signaling the bartender for another.

"Look," Watters said, "I've got a shitload of information for you." He pointed at an empty booth and picked up his bottle of beer. "Let's go over there. You've got to listen to me, and you've got to believe me."

"No," Bybee said, and he slowly shook his head back and forth like a mechanical toy. "No, no, no . . ."

Watters grabbed him by the arm. "Listen. I was probably wrong about her, about Zolene. Something's not right, but now I don't think she's involved. They watch her; they know she's got something. The other night, I saw a fucking Nav sneaking around her house—"

Bybee suddenly slammed his fist down on the bar and slid off the stool, trying to stand and face Watters, but he stumbled against the bar and held on to it with one hand.

"So now you're spying, you've . . . changed the players," Bybee said. His voice was loud, slurred, and the bartender approached again, this time motioning to someone across the room. "Now it's . . . Navs and Sipes and"—he waved his hand around the bar and then pointed at the bartender—"this guy and . . . that guy over there. . . ."

"Brig," Watters said, "you've got to listen to me."

". . . but not Zolene anymore." Bybee laughed and pushed his glasses back along his nose. "Ain't that a kick in the ass? Not Zolene."

"Brig, you're probably going to have to try this case alone." Watters withdrew the folded notepaper from his pocket and held it out to Bybee. "Take this. Read it when you sober up. It summarizes everything; it tells you what to do, who to call as witnesses, experts—everything, the exhibits. You'll need the map that's—"

"Witnesses? Zolene a witness? No . . . not Zolene anymore. No, no. That was just a little mistake. . . ."

He put both hands out and tried to shove Watters from his stool, but Watters easily fended him off and pushed Bybee away instead, sending the bar stool clattering across the floor. He snatched up one of Bybee's hands and slapped the wad of papers into it, like a process server, and folded his fingers over it.

"Read it!" Watters yelled.

"Stick it up your ass."

Watters grabbed Bybee's arm. "You ignorant fuck. Do you

know why you were appointed to this case? Because they knew you were shell-shocked, my friend. They knew you wouldn't dare try to do anything fucking weird again, like with the Sipes case. They wanted you here because they knew you'd glide, Bybee-style, and just half-ass it. They set you up too, man."

"Fuck you!" Bybee yelled.

The bartender came up with Bybee's drink, set it down, and motioned to a man across the room.

"Outside," the bartender said. "Now."

In a few seconds, a tall, paunchy cowboy with a beard appeared at Bybee's side, and he waited, his thick hands on his hips. Watters pulled several bills from his pocket and tossed them on the bar, then he walked to the door and left. Bybee began to follow, then stopped in the middle of the floor, but the big cowboy came up behind him. The loud music still ground away, but the pool players had stopped and were watching them, holding their cues across their chests like rifles.

"Okay," Bybee said. "Okay, okay." He waved the folded notes in the air and walked to the door and went outside.

Watters had lit up a cigarette, and now he stood next to the metal cowboy, smoking, and looked out toward the dark, gloomy cliffs to the east. Bybee shuffled past him and made his way unevenly to his car, then fumbled in his pocket for his keys, still holding the notes.

"Give me a ride?" Watters said. "Back to town, to the sheriff's office. Might as well get this shit over with."

Bybee leaned against the car and squinted through the darkness. Even in his stupor, and in the weak lights outside the Buckskin, he could see that Watters was frightened, defeated—and he vaguely enjoyed it.

"No," Bybee said. "I don't want to see you anymore." He laughed, suddenly. "That's just what she said: *I don't want to see you anymore.* So long . . . *my friend.*"

"Read those notes," Watters yelled.

Bybee climbed into the car, started it, and slowly drove out of the lot and back onto the highway. In his side mirror, he had one last glimpse of Watters standing next to the metal cowboy, cigarette smoke billowing up around him as though his head were on fire.

He weaved down the highway, and when he crossed the state line, he pulled over at a small rest area and, leaning out the window, tossed Watters's notes into a trash barrel.

Two hours later Bybee awoke in his car, half collapsed against the passenger side door, one long leg on the seat and the other hanging over to the floor. Slowly he struggled upright and looked through the windows. He was on the side of a highway, far off on the shoulder, and around him, everywhere, were towering, chalky bluffs, eerie and glowing, like the mountains on the moon.

He straightened completely and shook his head, trying to right himself, and finally reasoned he had driven north from Kanab into the heart of the Grand Staircase, the land of the White Cliffs, before he had pulled over and passed out. Although the moon was up, it was a dark, thick night, and the highway where he sat was deserted.

He belched—long and hard, nearly retching—and his head began to throb. He felt sick, and he leaned his head back and let the nausea pass, and then sat up again. Instinctively, he checked that his wallet was in his pocket, his watch still on his wrist, and then he turned on the weak dome light and inspected his face in the rearview mirror. As he suspected, it was a mess, smeared with mucus and spittle, his glasses askew, and he wiped his hand across his mouth.

In front of him, at a distance, he saw headlights, and he started the engine, turned on his lights, sat erect, and waited for the car to pass. After it drove by, he made a tight turn and headed south, his windows rolled down, and sucked in the cool air that washed over him.

Fifteen minutes later, he was out of the Whites and into the next tier, the Vermilion Cliffs, the red sandstone now purple against the black sky. The highway was deserted and quiet, the humming of his engine the only sound as he zigzagged down the valley past the turnoff to the Coral Pink Sand Dunes. It was a place he and Zolene had visited a week ago, a place where they had first clumsily held hands as she struggled across the dunes, laughing in the rosy sunlight, teasing him.

"Zolene," he said.

He knew what he would truly do now; he would go back to his tepee and shower, change clothes, and drive to her aunt's house. There he would humble himself—debase himself if he had to—and ask for her forgiveness. And she would give it, he was sure, maybe reluctantly, but he had seen her moods before, watched them swell and then recede like an emotional tide.

He was dizzy again, and fast becoming nauseous, the receding delirium of the liquor rising again, and he stopped the car and leaned his forehead against the steering wheel. His neck throbbed and his stomach felt hot and acidic, and he fumbled the door open and hunched sideways toward the highway, his head hanging.

But the vomit did not come, and he straightened, closed the door, and as he put the car in gear, saw in front of him and to the right a glint of moonlight on dark water. He drove the car forward and there, under a broad, yellowish cliff, he saw the lake—Three Lakes.

He continued along the shoulder until he could turn in to the bumpy entrance to the lake, and he drove back toward the cliff to the square of cement, where he parked and shut the engine off. He got out and leaned against his car, listening, straining to hear anything, maybe to hear her, the echo of her, but the canyon was tomblike, steeped in silence.

He walked to the edge of the water and stopped when black muck pulled at his shoes. He stepped away, staring out at the sheet of black water, a thing that she said had no bottom, that went straight to the middle of the earth, straight to hell.

Out of the corner of his eye, he saw something. It was floating on the dark surface, drifting, a log maybe, or part of an old raft. He leaned toward the water, squinting; there was something pale, familiar.

He squealed like an animal and began to twist away, but he

slipped and fell into the mud, and he crawled, desperate, until he was scrabbling along the rocks and dry dirt. He turned to see the thing again, floating; it was a man, half of his head submerged, his mouth and one eye open and staring, his blond hair splayed in thick tendrils across the water like a monstrous yellow spider clamped to his skull. His arms were spread, floating, as though he were balancing himself, readying himself to rise and stand in the mud and scream.

He looked harder now, squinting. Ronnie Watters.

Bybee turned and vomited—not just the liquor and bile that had been churning inside him, but a gush of horror, of black, watery death, of giant spiders and staring eyes, of a soundless scream from a dead mouth.

And then he ran. He picked himself up and ran from the edge of the lake to the highway, and then along the edge of the road toward town, his arms and legs flailing awkwardly, his feet heavy. He was stiff and slow, almost disjointed, unable to lope effortlessly as he usually could, and he tried to keep his head straight, his eyes locked forward, unseeing, his entire body clattering toward a line where a man waited—where many waited—their mouths opened to scream.

He ran. His breath came in explosive gulps, and his chest throbbed, and his legs began to tighten and ache, but he ran. He ran along the shoulder into the blackness until he tripped and went crashing into the gravel and tumbled, arms windmilling, into a ditch and lay, grunting in pain. But he struggled back to the road and ran, spittle and blood now streaking his face and neck.

A car approached him, slowed, and the driver's face appeared at the window like a mask, frightened, but Bybee ran on. The highway curved and seemed to widen, and he saw the outlying shacks and billboards, and then the giant arrowhead creaking in circles in the sky. He ran past the Piute Villa, past the frozen Indians and the crumbling cement tepees and finally the road bent eastward and he was on Center Street.

The town slept in the feeble, yellow glow of its streetlights, but the pavilion at the church still shone white, like a fire left blazing at the hearth. He ran directly toward it, straight down the middle of the street, his shoes slapping loudly at the pavement, echoing out to the cliffs. He was the only soul alive in the town; the rest were dead, all dead, all murdered and dumped in the lake, all floating, their mouths open, the water washing over them, drowning them, choking out their last desperate prayers.

He ran directly to the church, directly into the center of the light of glassed posters, and stopped and collapsed to his knees. The vomit burned in his throat and nose, and his eyes were smeared with sweat. His head pounded, and he felt himself swaying, losing his balance, falling from the cliffs, falling into a blackness. . . .

He lay on his back, his arms out to his side, and stared above him. His chest heaved and he felt the tightening in his stomach, the rising horror—

"Oh, Lord God," he said.

He was losing consciousness, and the church that loomed over him now seemed to be spinning, the lighted pictures of God and Jesus and all the Mormon saints blurring into a circling stream of fire, and he raised his head. He saw two bearded men in white robes, side by side, their hands extended to him. They were identical—mirror images of one another—and both were beckoning to him, urging him toward them as they stood, waiting.

He heard a rumbling, like thunder—a car—and a man's voice, deep and overpowering. And then he saw Zolene—Oh, God, Zolene! She was far away, somewhere in the rock-walled canyons, standing on a ledge, standing at the Indian Cave, streaked in blood and gore, naked, shouting to him across the dead fields to the Indian burial mounds that were now breaking open, spilling their rotted corpses, shouting to where he lay at the ranch among all the broken machines where the red earth had turned to blood and swept over him.

He floated in that sea of blood, dead, his eyes open, staring at the two identical men in robes who still waited, their arms outstretched.

11

HE had taken twenty deep breaths, and then he rose slowly, like a spirit, and all the LDS kids hushed themselves and watched. Daryl Pratt moved behind him and wrapped his arms around his chest and squeezed hard. His lanky body seemed to deflate and go limp, and he saw the sun spin through the cottonwood tree as he crumpled into the playground dirt.

He dreamed a long, strange dream about God and the Nephites and the Mormon pioneers, about a journey for centuries through dark tunnels and pale blossoms of light, the thrum of a great engine filling the universe as he bored straight through the darkness until he tumbled, free-falling, into the premortal world of the spirit babies, waiting.

And he dreamed of a beautiful woman with red hair.

Now he heard the voices, one far away and thin, and then a stronger, deeper voice, but he lay on his back, helpless under the cottonwood while the principal, Lavell Kirby, stood over him, his pink Mormon face working behind his glasses.

"Get up!"

The Squeeze had been outlawed in school.

"C'mon, man. Get up!"

Bybee opened his eyes and saw LeGrand Little's face hovering over him, his beard billowing around his face like a cloud, and he could smell food on his breath, something greasy.

"Get up."

But he lay on his back and listened to an electronic murmuring from somewhere, and a man's voice that the static swallowed and drowned. Behind it all was the sound of a truck or bus, its engine idling high and loud.

"C'mon, Bybee. Get up."

His left arm dangled beneath him on the cool floor, and his right arm was draped across his chest, over his heart, as though he were taking an oath. He smelled vomit—his vomit—splashed on his shirt and pants, and he tasted something bitter in his mouth—medicine, blood.

He finally sat up on the metal cot and looked around him at the windowless, yellow-painted walls, the open toilet, the metal door in the middle of a network of metal rods, woven together. LeGrand loomed directly in front of him, but behind him, in one corner of the cell, stood Lamar Little and Judge Mackleprang.

"Reed," Bybee said. His voice was weak, strained, as though it had not been used in years. Mackleprang, in gray slacks, a white shirt and tie, only nodded.

"Feel better?" LeGrand said.

Bybee put both hands to his neck, as though to keep his head from tumbling off, then looked at his clothes. He was splotched, head to toe, with mud and vomit, and his pants were torn at one knee and his shirt hung from him like a vest, two of the buttons ripped off.

"Where is this?" Bybee said. He raised his right hand and felt the dried blood at his nose and mouth, and he straightened his glasses, which were still intact, unbroken. "I saw a body—"

LeGrand did not answer, and the other two men moved around the cot so that they all stood in front of him. Lamar was in the middle—massive and woolly-bearded, his chest heaving under the uniform—while Mackleprang twisted his pale hands together and looked steadily at Bybee, at his blood-streaked face, the wild, muddy hair that hung in clumps.

"Why am I here?" Bybee said.

"Mr. Bybee," LeGrand said, "you are under arrest for the murder of Ronald Watters."

Bybee squinted at the deputy. "What?"

"You are under arrest for the murder of Ronald Watters," LeGrand said again. "You don't have to say anything, and if you want, we can get you a lawyer over to St. George." He pronounced it "Jarge."

"What the hell are you talking about?"

He stood up, a tall, wretched creature in tatters, like a shipwreck survivor, but LeGrand pushed him back down on the cot.

Bybee turned to Mackleprang; his heart was thumping now, and he could feel the heat in his face, the familiar panic. "Reed, what the hell is going on? I saw Watters at the lake. I found him."

"Brig," Mackleprang said, "just stay quiet." His chin had a small bandage pasted to it, and he looked truly troubled. "Stay quiet and listen."

"Listen to what? This crazy shit? I didn't kill Watters."

LeGrand stepped back and made room for his father, and the sheriff shuffled forward, breathing heavily and noisily, his beard only inches from Bybee's nose.

"Now, Reed's right," Lamar said. His voice rumbled from deep within him, as though he were slowly forcing the words up from the very depths of him. "Just stay quiet and listen to me."

"This is crazy," Bybee said.

The sheriff nodded. "The clark over to the Piute Villa says you and Watters argued hard the other night. About a woman, it seems."

"That was because—"

Lamar held up his hand, a good traffic cop stopping the rush. "You just listen. Than, over to the Buckskin Tavern, bartender says you and Watters was fightin' again last night. And you war drunk, he says. Had to throw both you boys out."

Bybee's hands began to tremble, and he shook his head. Outside, the whine of the truck engine grew louder, higher pitched.

"Than, last night," the sheriff went on, "a man named Jared Smoot seen you running down the Long Valley highway, all tore up and scared looking." He nodded his big, shaggy head at his son. "Than me and LeGrand find you passed out over to the church, muddied up, bloody, looking like you been in a heck of a scrape."

"Look—"

"And your car's over to Three Lakes whar we find Watters, drownded."

"This is crazy," Bybee said. He looked at LeGrand and then at Mackleprang, dimly realizing now that a judge, a neutral magistrate, should have no part of something like this, standing shoulder to shoulder with the police. "I'm being set up."

LeGrand laughed, but his father half turned and pointed a finger at him, silencing him.

Lamar turned back to Bybee. "Wol, we got enough evidence to go to the judge," he said, and he nodded at Mackleprang. "Get an information signed. File a case."

Bybee pounded his fist on his leg. "For Christ's sake, I didn't kill Watters!" He turned to Mackleprang, his dark eyes unfocused, squinting. "Reed, tell them that this is nuts. You know me."

Mackleprang made the strange, pursing movement with his lips. "I'm sorry, Brig. This is bad; it really is."

Bybee began to stand again, but Lamar put his hand on his wide shoulder, stopping him. The spinning horror of it all began to seep into him, and he felt as if he were underwater—deep underwater—his head about to explode, the world darkening, ready to swallow him.

He took several deep breaths and listened to the screeching engine outside change pitch again, waver, then grow louder. The absurdity of it made him dizzy. His last criminal case that he had declared to himself a week ago would be his own, now, but as a defendant, framed, boxed, packaged, and shipped off to a Utah prison, like Parks, for something that he did not do. And it was all engineered by . . . what? By whom?

Bybee stared at Mackleprang. "This is the Daughter of Zion, isn't it, Reed? Watters had this one figured out."

Lamar laughed, a deep, phlegmy clearing of his chest, and his son grinned. "You read too many books," Lamar said. "Thar's no such thing."

Bybee hung his head and stared at the dirty cement floor. He tried to order his thoughts, tried to reconstruct the last two weeks and, especially, the last twenty-four hours, to fashion a plausible explanation, a rationale for everything—a defense. But his head—his whole body—throbbed, and he could not think, not argue, not find a single, simple exit.

"Thar is a way out of all this, though," Lamar said.

"What?"

"Thar's a way you can keep from going to jail. A way you can get back home."

"What are you talking about?" Bybee said.

The sheriff went to the door of the cell and looked down the short hallway, ensuring that Marla did not lurk there, that they were out of earshot of any other prisoner. He came back and stood in front of Bybee.

"You got a trial in two days," he said, and he tilted his big head toward the hallway, presumably to where Parks was caged.

"Not anymore," Bybee said.

"Yeah, you do," Lamar said. "Everyone is going to trial—you and Hightower and Reed and Parks. Everyone."

"I don't understand you," Bybee said.

"All you boys go to trial and you put on a regular case, just like always. You let Hightower put on all his evidence and his witnesses; you object and cross-examine and do what all you defense lawyers do."

Bybee looked at Mackleprang; it was beginning to make sense. "A standard trial," he said.

Lamar smiled. "Wol, that's right. Standard. You don't start up with all that nonsense that Watters probably told you and was spouting off about to Reed the other night. You know, the Navs lying and me and LeGrand doing something wrong. All that."

"In other words, roll over," Bybee said. "Play dead."

"Wol, yeah. You sit thar in a coat and tie with Parks and you do your lawyer stuff and act like you usually do. You do what Reed, har, says you usually do, just stay calm. But you let the jury put Parks away. Than, you—"

"This is bullshit."

"Than," Lamar went on, holding up his hand, "you talk to your girlfriend and you get that document she has and you give it to me. She knows what it is. Probably you, too, I imagine. And—"

"She doesn't know any—"

"—than we don't say nothing about murder. Everyone around har thinks Watters just drownded, and that's the way we'll let it be, an accident. We drop everything."

"Just like that."

"Just like that," Lamar echoed.

Bybee sat stock-still and looked at the man. To most of the locals, he guessed, Lamar Little was simply a small-town sheriff, a shuffling fat cop who handed out parking tickets. But to others, he realized, he was a uniformed Buddha, a slob savant, a big, brooding man whose mysterious silence seemed to envelope Kanab, to protect it, even to symbolize it. He was like their demi-prophet, their sub-seer, a man who communicated with the higher powers and demanded answers in return.

"Zolene won't speak to me anymore," Bybee said.

"Wol, I think she will now," the sheriff said. "Lot at stake."

"I won't do it."

"Yeah, you will," Lamar said. He waved his chubby hand, pointing. "You been in too many places like this not to know you don't want to spend the rest of your life thar. Besides, a war hero like you—"

"I'm not a war hero!"

Lamar grinned. "Wol, maybe not."

Bybee closed his eyes to keep the room from spinning, the nausea from welling up. He felt exactly as he had at Fort Rucker when he received his orders to Vietnam—the only American in his entire graduating flight class to be sent there. But back then, the chances of ending up dead or maimed or in a VC tiger cage were about 50 percent. Now a similar fate was almost certain, the deck stacked.

"How can I trust you?" Bybee said. "What's to keep you from getting what you want, and then putting both Parks *and* me away?"

The sheriff laughed again and held out his hands like a preacher. "Wol, you just got to have faith, Mr. Bybee. War honorable men."

"Right," Bybee said.

His head still ached, and he felt out of breath, but he closed his eyes and concentrated. Watters had been right, all along. Parks was innocent, and these men in front of him—and others, no doubt—were truly a secret posse, vigilantes. And Watters had gone babbling about it to the judge, with Sipes hearing it all and, because of what he knew, had been murdered—smothered or choked, held under water until he died—and then left floating in the weeds and muck.

And Zolene. Watters, at the Buckskin, had said something about a Navajo stalking her, and Bybee knew of the earlier incident at the ranch. There was a weakness in all of this, a missing piece of the puzzle, and Zolene obviously held that piece, the answer.

And now she was his only hope, he realized; he had to have the document—whatever it was.

"Okay," Bybee said. "I'll do it."

Mackleprang smiled, relieved, and Lamar slapped Bybee on the back, making a hollow, thumping sound. "We have a deal, than."

He motioned toward the door, LeGrand opened it, and Bybee stood, slowly, his head nearly scraping the low ceiling of the cell. LeGrand and Lamar and Mackleprang moved out of the cell into the hallway, and Bybee looked around him, as though he were checking out of a hotel room, searching for stray belongings, and then walked out.

"Down thar," Lamar said, and he pointed to another door. "We got your wallet and things. Your car's outside, too."

Dutifully, Bybee followed the three of them down a long hallway toward the sound of a police radio, the static now loud and buzzing, like a giant insect. On either side of the hallway were four more cells, each with the webwork of heavy rods and a solid door in the middle. All were empty except one, the last one, where a boy, clean-shaven with short blond hair, unevenly cut, sat on the cot and watched them pass.

"Mr. Bybee," he said.

Bybee stopped and stared at the boy, then realized that it was Owen Parks. Without his long hair and beard, he looked like a high school student, adolescent, baby-faced—and scared out of his wits.

Parks stood up and came to the webwork, his eyes red and sore. Behind him, on the floor, was a yellow starburst of dried vomit.

"Mr. Bybee, I heard them talking this morning. Ronnie is dead, isn't he?"

Bybee nodded and looked down at the boy. "Yes."

Parks hung his head. "Oh, God."

"Let's go," LeGrand said.

"I need to talk to my client," Bybee said.

"Wol, you got one minute," LeGrand said, and he walked out the door where the other two men had just exited.

Bybee turned back to Parks and put his hand on the boy's fingers, which clutched the webbing like claws. Behind him, on the cot, lay a powder blue sport coat, a bow tie, brown shoes, and a white shirt—the ill-fitting hayseed clothes Watters had promised.

"How are you, Owen?" Bybee said. He looked back down the hallway at the cell he had just vacated; he knew the boy had not heard what just went on. "You okay?"

Parks's face was a cadaverous white, worse than the usual jailhouse pallor, and he was twitching, oblivious to Bybee's torn, mud-caked clothes and his bloodied face. "No," he said.

"Owen—"

"Do you think I'm guilty, Mr. Bybee?"

Bybee said nothing. He squeezed Parks's fingers, and then the boy closed his eyes and began to cry, pressing the top of his head against the webbing.

"I didn't do it, Mr. Bybee."

Bybee stepped away and watched the boy cry, then he turned his back and walked to the door.

"Mr. Bybee?"

He opened the door, dipping his tall frame through the opening, and then closed it, leaving Parks alone.

✦

As Bybee pulled away from the sheriff's office, he rolled down the windows of his car and sucked in air like a man surfacing from the depths of a black pool—from a bottomless lake. He drove automatically, by instinct, taking the familiar route to Zolene's house through the quiet backstreets. A few children played in the cool, shady yards, a man worked in his garden, a woman sat on a porch—all oblivious to the terror in their little town that seethed beneath them, beside them, all around them.

He pulled up in front of Mrs. Frost's house, and at the irrigation ditch he washed his face and arms, the back of his neck, and slicked his hair smooth. He still looked battered, ragged, but he mounted the steps to the porch and rang the bell.

Orma Frost answered, and Bybee stood in front of her, towering above her, desperate and pleading, begging to see Zolene. In his torn slacks and white shirt, he looked like a tramp, a reverse missionary preaching chaos and ruin, a retreat to the devil, and Mrs. Frost refused to let him in. Zolene was gone, she told him; she had packed her things and driven away, leaving only a simple note behind.

Bybee thanked her and walked away from the house and stood by the ditch, studying his watch. It was midafternoon; if he left now, he could arrive in Tucson by midnight, and maybe by tomorrow morning, he would have talked to her and reconciled everything, and he would have the document . . . or know where it was.

But he needed food and a shower, rest, and he drove to the IGA, bought a can of soda and cellophaned sandwiches, and returned to the Piute Villa. He walked inside his tepee and saw immediately that the place had been searched—clothes torn from closets and drawers, bedding tossed aside, even his shaving kit emptied on the floor. Without bothering to try and restore the room to some sort of order, he stripped off his clothes and stood under a hot shower until, like the other day, when he was thinking of Zolene, it ran cold.

He toweled himself dry and then sat cross-legged on the

naked mattress and slowly ate his sandwiches and sipped at the soda, his eyes fixed on the sloping walls. After he finished his food, he grew sleepy, and he took off his glasses and put the unfinished soda aside, setting it atop the bedside *Book of Mormon.*

He slept, and he resumed the dream he had awoken with in the jail, but then it gave way to a vision of Moroni, the last Nephite, wounded and bleeding, cradling his gold plates as he sought a place for them, somewhere deep in the hills, away from the enemies that would kill for them . . . a hiding place. . . .

. . . and then Sipes appeared, as he always did—thick and naked and hairless, with a cock that writhed, pale and wet, like a snake, up from his crotch and around his head. . . .

12

IN Hell's Bellows, darkness does not descend, as the writers like to say; it is not the result of the whirring and dodging of the planet, the cosmic pulsing of light and shadow, sunrise and sunset, some phenomenon from above. Rather, it comes from below; it unfolds from the red sand like a black blossom that grows upward, rising and spreading until it envelops the land and squeezes out the last desperate tentacles of light.

And there it remains, something living and palpable, smothering all existence as it lies humped, almost breathing.

Zolene sat on the front porch of the ranch house, submerged in this darkness, staring past the wrecked machines toward the apple orchard, toward Lamb's house, toward another dimension of darkness. Above her, the sky was so black, so clear, that the Milky Way lay smeared, horizon to horizon, like a stain.

Before she left town, she had bought a six-pack of beer at Lloyd Honey's Texaco—a dark, expensive brand in green bottles—and now she slowly drank one, letting each cold swallow trickle down her throat. Her car was nearby, gassed, her luggage inside, ready for the trip across the reservations and over the mountain at Flagstaff, then down into the desert and the purifying heat—and away from all this. But she could not leave; something tugged at her, rooted her here.

"Doug," she said.

She drank and then held the bottle out toward the field of

weeds and dirt, the same field from where her mother had once come running, two decades ago, when it was rich, green alfalfa, crying and ripping off a straw hat and bandanna as Doug stood at his tractor and cursed after her.

"Hey!"

She stood now, and raised the bottle like a kerosene lamp, the kind she used to read by in the basement when the generator failed, as though it could spread a thin light into the field, into the past.

"Hey, Doug!"

She lifted the bottle higher, and the field began to dimly glow, and in one corner, by the wooden cattle guard, by the road to Wester Lewis's place, she could barely make out her grandfather. He was bent over the long mower arm, and the tractor still throbbed behind him as he ripped the wet tendrils from the fouled blades.

"Hey, it's me, Doug," she yelled. "Zoley. I have to talk to you—"

The field brightened, and she could now see the dull red paint on the tractor and Farnsworth's blue work shirt, and in that eerie glow the old man looked up from the mower and stared at her, the sharp features on his face accented by the yellowish light.

"Zoley?"

"Yeah, it's me," she said. "C'mon, tell me."

The light began to fade, and Farnsworth took off his baseball cap and walked away from the mower, toward her. He was going to tell her; he was going to come out of the field, wash up, and sit down at the dining room table like he always did, smelling of soap, his hair watered and combed, his false teeth clicking in his mouth. He would tell her.

But he stopped.

"Zoley."

The light flickered and dimmed, and he pointed at the hills to the east, toward the Indian Cave, then he was gone, the night black again.

Zolene lowered the empty bottle and began to cry.

✦

The next morning, Bybee bumped along the road into the ranch, and as he passed the collapsed silo, he saw the glint of white in the hills. He pulled the car off the road, got out, and set off for the cliffs, for the white spot there.

Although it was still early morning, the sun was warm, and the hum of flies and the cawing of birds filled the air as he walked. He was dressed in a yellow knit shirt and blue jeans, still stiff and starchy, and he took long, deliberate strides up the hill. By degrees, the white spot materialized into a shape, a woman, the same way she had dissolved, piece by piece, the last time he saw her.

He clambered over the last jumble of rocks and a row of scrub pine and came up to the ledge in front of the Indian Cave. Zolene sat on the same flat rock she had rested upon several days ago, dressed how Bybee would always remember her, how he would paint her if he were an artist: tight jeans, a sleeveless white blouse, silver earrings dangling at the side of her white face—and her hair . . . wild and uncombed, framing her face with fire.

"Hello," Bybee said.

"Hello, Brig," she said. The wind on the ledge was as strong as it had been the other day, and she turned so that her hair blew away from her face.

"I thought you had gone home," he said.

She smiled and looked past him, out over the canyon and the red cliffs. "I am home."

"I guess so."

"I heard about Watters. I'm sorry. It's awful."

"He was murdered, Zolene."

She lifted her head, and he could see that her face was lined, the eyes tired. "I know," she said, "or I guessed that. They say he drowned; that he was drunk and tried to go swimming. But I know better."

"The sheriff has charged me with his murder. Or he's going to."

She put her hand to her face, and her eyes grew wide and round. "Oh, God."

"I didn't do it, and they know that. They're blackmailing me. They'll drop everything if I go to trial tomorrow and look the other way while Parks is convicted."

"Brig—"

"And if I give them the document your grandfather was hiding."

Zolene did not say anything, but continued to look out over the canyon, at the cars and trucks speeding along the highway, miles away, soundless, the world rushing by this place, oblivious to it.

"Parks is innocent, Zolene. Whoever murdered Watters murdered your grandfather. You must realize that by now."

She turned her face away from the wind again, and Bybee walked over to the rock and sat next to her, his knees high, his arms draped over them. "The night he was killed, Watters talked to me," he said. "He told me that he knew your grandfather went to Salt Lake just before he was killed to sell whatever he had been hiding on this ranch to the church, to Bellard Sipes."

Zolene still looked away. "And you believe that, too?"

"Yes, Zolene, I do. I'm sorry, but I do." He finally put his hand on her shoulder and gently turned her so that she looked into his face—a face as drawn as hers, as troubled, and eyes that seemed sadder, darker, the pain evident. "But Watters made one thing clear the last time he talked to me, Zolene. He knows you had nothing to do with it." He hesitated, then reached out and took her hand; she did not pull it back. "I know that, too, and I'm sorry. I really am. I truly am."

Zolene nodded and squeezed his hand, and he could feel her relax and soften.

"I guess he—both of you," she said, "had a right to be suspicious." She pulled strands of hair from her face. "Brig, I'm just trying to save this." She pointed at the ranch below them, at the primitive, almost untouched beauty of the whole canyon—the red cliffs, the sea of sage, the timeless serenity of it all.

"What do you mean?"

"My uncle Carl hated this place—I told you that. Doug knew that, too, so he rewrote his will a few years ago and left it all to me. But Carl wanted to develop this canyon, make a retirement village. He wanted to subdivide, bring in water and sewage and cable TV, pave the road, even put in a golf course, swimming pool. Jesus, probably a gas station and grocery store." She looked at him. "Brig, this is the most isolated place in the world; it's beautiful, untouched; that's why they used to make movies around here. But Carl wants to destroy it; he wants to make it a suburb, fill this canyon up with houses and cars and noise."

Bybee smiled. "Make Kanab a city, this a suburb."

"Yes."

"And that's why he challenged the will."

"Yes. He claims that Doug had gone . . . crazy, had lost his mind, and that he didn't know what he was doing when he rewrote the will."

"But why would you have to lie about everything?"

"Because the truth made Doug sound like he really *was* crazy, Brig. I didn't want Watters or anyone snooping around, that's why I told him I didn't know who owned the place. I didn't want to get into all this about the will and Carl's lawsuit, and everything else. Doug was broke and needed money bad, but if people knew that he claimed he had some secret document and was trying to sell it to the church, he would be branded as a kook, another Freddy Crystal, and it would help Carl prove his case." She waved her hand at the ranch again. "And this would be called Johnson Canyon Estates in a few years, or Vermilion Acres—something like that."

"So you went to Salt Lake with him?"

"Yes—no, not with him. I got a letter from Doug a few days before Thanksgiving last year, telling me what he was going to do. I panicked and left the kids with a friend, drove to the airport, and flew to Salt Lake and rented a car. I wanted to stop all this. I finally found him at his motel, but it was too late; he had already gone to the church headquarters to see Bellard Sipes. He was angry, yelling about . . . things. Sipes had told him to go to hell, that the document was a fake, that Doug was nuts. Doug drove back here on Thanksgiving morning, and I followed him in the rental car. We got here right about noon; I stayed a bit and then drove on, got hung up in Flagstaff in some snow, and didn't get back to Tucson until late at night."

"But you knew Parks wasn't here then, on Thanksgiving afternoon?"

"No. I left just after noon. They said Doug was killed around five o'clock. I had no reason to doubt that. Parks could have come out here then."

"Or somebody else," he said.

For several moments they were silent, and Bybee idly tossed rocks over the ledge and listened to them as they clattered on the boulders below. The wind scattered his hair around his head, and he mechanically reached up every few moments and forced it back.

"Zolene," he finally said. "Sipes is here, in Kanab."

"What?"

"The other night, when Watters went busting into Judge Mackleprang's motel room, he found Sipes there. And yesterday, when I was in the jail, Mackleprang was there, with the sheriff. Sipes probably wasn't too far away, either. Watters was right; there is a posse, a secret organization. The Daughter of Zion." Bybee moved closer to her. "Watters also told me in the beginning that this case was soaked in Mormon secrets, and he was right, wasn't he?"

"Yes," she said. Her eyes were wet now, her lower lip trembling. "I knew about *something* when I was little, Brig, I just didn't know what it was . . . or where it was." She smoothed a tear away from her cheek and bent her head back to the blue sky. "Until now."

"Where is it?"

She pointed at the deep gap in the two large boulders near them—the Indian Cave. "No one ever knew about this spot, Brig. But once, when I was a kid, I got stranded up here in the rain—a bad one, like the other day. Doug saw me and hiked up to help me back down. I showed him my secret hiding place, and he looked at it and laughed. Then last night I realized that this is where it was—is." She pointed at the tiny cave again. "See for yourself; I found it this morning."

Bybee got up and moved to the mouth of the hole and, on all fours, peered inside. There, in the damp gloom, against the farthest rock, lay a green plastic trash bag, tied and folded. He reached in and dragged it out into the daylight.

"Open it," Zolene said.

Bybee did as he was told; he unfastened the loose knot and pulled out a dried, leather valise. It was scarred, part of it blackened and burned, and the metal snaps and buckles were rusted, some of them broken. He opened it and found an old Bible, a large family edition, bound in black leather with faint gold letters on the bottom that read *Josiah Lamb*.

"Inside the Bible," Zolene said.

Bybee opened the book and pulled out a folded piece of paper. It was brittle and yellowed, stained by water, and one side of it was filled with smeared, black handwriting. It was an old letter—undeniably old—and it nearly separated at the creases as he opened it. He glanced at the date at the top, the signature at the bottom, then read the letter through—read it again—and when he finished, he folded it and put it back inside the Bible.

"Lord God," he said.

"That's what Doug was murdered for," she said. "Watters, too."

Bybee stared at the Bible. "And Sipes wasn't going to spend any church money for it," he said, "but he was going to destroy it, one way or another."

"Yes."

He slipped the Bible, with the letter inside, back into the leather valise and closed it. He stared at the ground for a moment, the blurry memory of all the old boyhood ghost stories and the whispered horrors alive now, true. He walked back to the rock, sat down, and put his arm around her, and she relaxed and leaned against him. They remained this way for several minutes, clinging to one another, trying to dispel a coldness, feeling the closeness of each other the way they had just a few days before—years before.

And as he held her, he tried to concentrate on the two of them, the sweep of the red countryside around them, the hard blue sky. But he could only see one thing, one person—Owen Parks clinging to the webbing in his cell, sobbing, the reek of vomit and fear swirling around him.

He shifted and took both of his hands in hers, facing her, and kissed her on the cheek. "I have to go, Zolene." He pointed at the valise and stood up. "And I need that. "

Zolene hung her head. "Oh God, Brig. You just said that Parks is innocent."

"I need that," Bybee said again.

Suddenly Zolene extended her leg and violently kicked the valise with her foot. "Then *take* the damned thing, Brig! Burn it, for all I care!"

Bybee picked up the valise, took the Bible from it, and tucked it under his arm. Zolene stood up, and as she did, the wind blew her hair across her face, masking her. She cleared it away, and Bybee leaned in to her, trying to kiss her again, but she drew back. Her eyes were wet, one tear coursing down her cheek.

"Mountain Meadows, Brig," she said, and she pointed at the Bible. "It will never end."

13

MOUNTAIN MEADOWS, UTAH
SEPTEMBER 13, 1857, 2:21 P.M.

The man on the horse returns the salute as John Lee approaches on foot and stops.

—Let me speak to them again, Brother Higbee. They mean us no harm.

Higbee leans forward in his saddle, making it creak and groan as though a man thrice his weight sits upon it. The hide of the horse quivers, and its bulging black eyes look straight out at the encircled wagons below it.

—They've abused our women and stole goods right in Pinter. They've shamed us. Is that not enough?

—It is wrong, brother.

—And it is wrong, Brother *Lee, to boast of killing the Prophet; to boast of killing us all.*

Something startles the horse, and its head jerks upward.

—Damn. Keep your Indians down, John.

Lee looks back over his shoulder at the three Indians squatting near them, and then farther still, at a place where nearly one hundred of them hide and wait. They are dark and dirty and dressed in white man's clothes; some call them the battle-ax of the Lord.

—They says they have the pistol that killed Joseph Smith, another man says. He has drooping blond hair and holds a wooden

cane, and he lounges on the ground as casually as a man might at a Sunday outing.

Higbee nods. —Ay, they mean us harm.

—But yet they haven't, and so we move in haste, Lee says.

—We are placed upon the anvil. If Buchanan's army won't do it, these Gentile bastards will. I swear they will.

Lee points at the encampment. —There are children down there.

—And there were children at Haun's Mill, Higbee says.

Lee turns away and looks out across the narrow valley, where the emigrants have huddled behind embankments and their wagons amid the waving grass and scrub oak near the seeps. A fire burns somewhere in their camp, and the thin, grayish smoke curls upward until it is printed, undissolved, against the blue of the Utah sky.

Higbee stares at Lee for several moments and then spits into the ground. —Damn you, John, if you haven't the stomach for this.

A man rides over the small rise behind them and gallops up to Higbee, forcing Lee to step back. His horse is wet and laboring and a yellowish foam drips from its mouth. The rider, a man named Haslam, hands over a battered leather pouch, and Higbee quickly pries it open and turns away. After a moment, he swivels back to Lee.

—The plan will be put into effect, John.

Lee holds up one hand, as though stopping the words. —Then I am through praying, brother. I act only as an instrument now.

—Call yourself what you will. Tell your Indians to pass the word and keep down. Remember your duty.

Higbee turns to another man close by, leans toward him across the neck of his horse, and hands him the leather pouch. —Brother Lamb, take this away and destroy it.

Lamb nods, and Higbee straightens and turns again to Lee. —Just mind what you are about, John. Ask for Fancher.

Lee hesitates and then turns to the young man—a boy —who sits on the ground, absently twisting a white kerchief that he has fastened to his cane.

—You know what to do, Brother Bateman? To say?

—Yes, sir.

—Then let's be about it. Hold that thing high.

With the cane thrust before them, Lee and Bateman walk down the slope toward the train of wagons and mules and cattle, slipping at times on the tall grass. As they draw nearer, a white flag from the camp suddenly appears, held aloft on a long rod above the tops of the wagons, and the two stop. After a moment, they struggle through the mud of the seeps and walk into the circle of wagons.

Minutes later, Lee emerges and looks back up the hill.

—God forgive us, he whispers, and he waves his arm at Higbee.

Higbee waves his arm in return. —Every man on his feet. Each of you will accompany one walking male. Do your duty.

The men sprawled across the grass, about fifty in number, stir and then rise to their feet. They are farmers, ranchers, simple merchants from Cedar City and the small surrounding settlements—all Saints, all priests within the church, men bent under the will of the Heavenly Father who await their celestial glory.

The men walk slowly, tiredly, behind two of their own empty wagons that creak toward the encampment where Lee now stands. When they arrive, some of the Mormons begin helping about a dozen wounded emigrants—pale and stumbling, bandages dripping from them—into the wagons. They lie back, collapsing, and are crowded together, almost stacked like sacks of grain, until the wagons are full. A limp hand droops over a side board, a leg, black and gangrenous, juts out above another, and bloodied hands flutter to faces to block the afternoon sun.

The other men in the camp, those not wounded, begin to file out from between the wagons and assemble there. They are battered and dirty and unarmed, and some are stained with the blood of those lying in the wagons. The Mormon men who have tramped down the slope each find a man and stand next to him, shoulder to shoulder, until the entire company is duly formed: a long, dirty line facing north, two men abreast, one Mormon standing to the right of one Gentile.

The wagons carrying the wounded rattle slowly ahead, and about two hundred feet from the emigrant camp it stops, and Lee hurries between them and then gestures toward the interior of the camp. Slowly, with only the sound of skirts rustling against the sage and grass and the coughing from fevered throats, the women and children emerge and gather in a mass behind the wagons and ahead of the odd line of their husbands and fathers. They are as filthy as their men, but some of the women and older girls have hastily arranged their hair in neat buns and reddened their cheeks, and the boys have dampened their hair and scraped their boots clean of mud and manure. Mothers hush some of the smaller children and poke at the older ones, and a few of the girls look shyly under bonnets or scarves at the younger Mormon men, who now stand protectively next to their fathers. But the men only look away and stare back up the slope at Higbee, who has his arm upraised.

For a moment, all is still. The coughing stops and the children cease their murmuring, and all of the souls gathered in this place called Mountain Meadows thank God for their deliverance.

Lee sees Higbee's arm drop, and at the same time he turns to watch a woman take off her bonnet and lift her face to the pure blue of the sky.

—Do your duty, he shouts.

Each Mormon man marching with one of the men from the camp steps to the side and withdraws his pistol from his belt or pocket, places it against the head of the man to his left, and fires a bullet into his skull. Most of the men crumple, dead before they hit the ground, but others stand, blinking in horror, as their guards, refusing to comply with the order, fire their pistols into the air and move away from the killing and kneel in the grass.

At the moment the first volley is fired, the Indians who had waited north of the encampment rise and swoop down upon the women and children. The mothers shriek and gather the little ones to them and begin to run to the west, but the axes of the Indians chop them down. The infants and smaller children are spared, but the others, the older ones, scream as the Indian blades slash their throats and rip open their stomachs.

The Mormon men driving the wagons of wounded rise from their seats and begin shooting into the mass of bandaged men writhing on the dusty boards. Hands that had sought to shield faces from the sun now extend to stop the bullets. Lee too has withdrawn his gun, and he stands between the two wagons and tips it over the edge of each wagon in turn, firing into the screaming mass.

The sounds of death fill the meadow. Those still alive, those who twist and moan in bloody piles, are instantly axed into silence by the Indians or shot by the Mormons who prowl through the sweep of slaughter like men working a field. The Saints who refused to shoot a Gentile man in the head—six of them—are still gathered at one side of the meadow, where they kneel and pray, while two of their group bawl out loud.

On the western side of the encampment, two young girls have escaped the massacre, but an Indian on horseback quickly runs them down and brings them back to the killing. They are the last survivors other than the babies and small children that have been spared, and they are brought to Higbee, who has ridden down from the hill, shooting into any body that he sees twitch.

One girl, in a blue dress streaked with blood, sobs wildly, but the other, a taller, red-haired girl in a thick green skirt, stares at the sky, waiting. Higbee dismounts, walks up to the two women, and forces them to kneel before him. He presses his crotch into the face of one and then cups her breast and squeezes it until she screams.

—They are so pretty, brother, he says to the man next to him, and then he walks behind them and fires a bullet into the backs of their necks.

All of the Saints have stopped now, and they stand sweating, smeared with the gore of children and women on their trousers. Lee has taken charge of the survivors—eighteen children too young to talk—and he herds them farther north into the scrub oak, away from the mutilated bodies of their parents. The children huddle around each other and cling to the oldest in the group and then, slowly, like a wind, a wailing rises from them, from all of them, as they sense their desolation, and they turn to Lee, who begins to sob with them.

The word is given, and the looting begins. Watches and money are snatched from pockets, spectacles yanked away from dead eyes, ringed fingers hacked off, and finally, clothes and shoes stripped away, leaving a field of naked bodies.

Others run back to the encampment, where the wagons sit undisturbed amid the domestic clutter of buckets and drying shirts, of water still boiling in kettles and a child's doll propped upright on a footboard. The livestock is quickly rounded up and led away and the wagons instantly torn apart. The Indians seize blankets, quilts, weapons, and clothing while the white men gather up clocks or dishes or lanterns, some even throwing portraits of persons they do not know—perhaps of those they have just murdered—into sacks that are then thrown over their shoulders. Tools, wooden spoons, ladles, books, a Bible, diaries, empty tins, empty kegs, stone crocks, a fiddle, soap, a music box, a churn, hats, a hen coop, yarn, toys—all are gathered up by the Saints and carried away.

A silence finally descends as the Mormons and Indians disappear. But one of them has dropped the music box in his haste to leave; the mechanism beneath the china lid comes to life and the weak, tinkling sound of a minuet drifts across the valley and floats away into the sky.

And then it stops, and Mountain Meadows is quiet again.

14

ABOUT a twenty-minute drive from Kanab, across the state line, lies the Arizona Strip, a stretch of dry, purplish scrubland that neither God nor government will touch, or has ever touched. It is a white man's reservation of sorts, a place of polygamy and persecution, a place that has withered into its own past.

At one edge of this strip sits a town once called Short Creek, a ramshackle polygamist community made of tin and tar paper and cinder blocks. In the early 1950s, during a lunar eclipse, dozens of federal deputies swept down on the town, dragging the wives screaming into the roads, while the children—all of them—were thrown into cars and vans and driven away into the darkness.

But during it all, the old, long-bearded Mormon men, the men the marshals were truly searching for, cowered in cellars and coal sheds, and finally scrambled north across the state line to Kanab, where they were hidden by friends.

And now and then around town, one of these "cohabs," one of these twisted practitioners of the faith, would appear. He could be seen, maybe, sitting at the rear of the church, or on someone's back porch, or even in one of the stores along Center Street, hollow-eyed and fanatical, out of place even in this odd little town of make-believe, where movies were once made.

At Lloyd Honey's Texaco, Bybee turned left—south, away from town—and drove toward the state line. In a matter of minutes he arrived at the roadway rest area where he had tossed Watters's notes. There was no one there, as before, and he pulled up, got out of his car, and opened the metal lid of the garbage can. It was empty; it had been dumped, and there was nothing there except a few beer cans at the bottom, resting on a clean plastic liner.

"Damn!"

He got back in his car and drove quickly back to town and into the parking lot of Parry Lodge. As he drove through the place, he saw that, on his left, the door to the Barry Sullivan Room was wide open, and inside, clothes and bedding were strewn everywhere.

He left his car near the Gary Cooper Room and, with the Bible under his arm, hurried across Center Street to the Book Outpost.

A bell tied to the brass handle jingled when the door opened, and an unhappy-looking woman in a dark skirt and dark sweater looked up at him from behind the counter. Her face was thin and acne-pitted, and her hair was pulled tightly back and tied behind her head. She did not acknowledge him, dropping her eyes to whatever she was reading.

Bybee stopped in the middle of the store and looked around him. In the rear, beyond the racks of postcards and bumper stickers and key chains, were row after row of books, neatly lined in shelves that extended from the floor almost to the ceiling. It was, as he had hoped, a religious bookstore, full of tracts for the eager and uninitiated: biographies of the prophets, histories of the church, confessionals, and on one shelf, the Bible, the *Book of Mormon*, the *Doctrine and Covenants*, and the *Pearl of Great Price*, all in separate editions or, at the end, all four in one volume—a fat, black cube of Mormon gospel.

"Can I help you?"

The clerk had walked up behind him, and now stood, her arms folded under her tiny breasts. She stared at the Bible in Bybee's hand, and he realized that she could probably read the words *Josiah Lamb* on the cover and he shifted his grip on it and turned it away.

"Yeah," he said, "I need a book on—"

He stopped; he saw the one he wanted, and he pulled out a large, thick book, with a photograph on its glossy cover. Tucking the Bible under his arm, Bybee leafed through the book, and in the middle, in the section usually reserved for photographs or charts or paintings, found what he needed.

"I'll take this," he said. He handed the book to the clerk and looked around him. "Do you have a copying machine?"

The woman looked again at his Bible. "Why?" she said.

"Because I need to make copies," Bybee said. "Oddly enough."

The woman hesitated, and for a moment Bybee thought she might suddenly turn and hurry to the rear and place a call, and in minutes LeGrand and his father would come roaring up.

"There," she said, and she pointed to a big gray machine in the corner, near the front. "Twenty-five cents a copy."

"Thanks," Bybee said.

While the clerk rang up the book, he walked to the machine and made sure his body shielded what he was about to copy. He fed a dollar into the mechanism, and after it warmed up, carefully took the fragile letter from the Bible and gently laid it on the glass. He closed the cover, punched the appropriate buttons, and waited while the light repeatedly swept across the document. When the machine had finished, he returned the letter and the copies to the Bible, and walked to the counter.

"You have envelopes? Stamps?" he said.

Again the woman hesitated, and then moved slowly, cautiously, as if a gun were trained on her, to another section of the counter. She returned with a box of letter-sized envelopes.

"Stamps are over there," she said, and she pointed to another machine at one side of the store.

Bybee paid, and without waiting for her to bag his purchases, took them and walked to the stamp machine. He bought several, and as he turned around, ready to leave, he heard the tiny bell jingling on the door handle. He looked up and saw a man walk in—muscular and thick-bodied, dressed in a business suit, his bald head glistening with sweat, his small mouth twisted. When he saw Bybee, he stopped and held out his hands.

"Well, counselor," he said. His voice had a muffled quality, as though his hand were in front of his mouth. "We meet again."

"Yeah, Sipes," Bybee said. "Unfortunately."

"Unfortunately," Sipes repeated. He took a step forward and extended a stubby hand, hairless and pale, something dead, exposing a monogrammed cuff, but Bybee kept his hands wrapped around his books and envelopes.

Sipes laughed and then bent forward, making a face, and tapped the cover of the Bible. "Finding the Lord, Mr. Bybee? At long last?"

"In a way," Bybee said. "Exorcism."

"Exorcism," Sipes said.

Bybee turned away, angry. It was the same technique Sipes had used throughout the trial during cross-examination, continually repeating what Bybee said or asked, making it seem in the end as if he were the honed and brilliant accuser, not the wretched accused.

Sipes bent forward again, staring, reading, his eyes lifeless and hard, like round stones, and pulled back. "Josiah Lamb? A friend of the family?"

"Yeah," Bybee said. "A good friend. Look, Bellard, it's been real nice."

"Real nice," Sipes said. He pointed at the other book with the glossy cover. "And this, too? Why the sudden interest? Shouldn't you be preparing for your big trial tomorrow? Another Bybee special?"

For an instant, Bybee considered shouting everything at the man, telling him in front of the clerk and the whole world about what he possessed, what he was about to do. But he realized what these men—and the squat, sweating, ugly man who stood in front of him, in particular—were capable of, what nightmares they had, and could, engineer.

Bybee felt his hands shaking. "Good-bye, Sipes."

He stepped around the man, walked to the door, and went outside. Near the store, parked next to the curb in a red-painted no-parking area, sat a new white Lincoln—a large luxury model—with the garish, chromed logo on the rear that Bybee recognized as that of a prominent Salt Lake City car dealership. As he started across the street, he heard the bell on the door again, and Sipes stood in the doorway, grinning, his dull, tiny teeth barely visible.

"Hey, Bybee," he yelled. "Say hello to Becky Chu when you see her. Nice girl."

Bybee stopped in the middle of the street and began to turn around, to rush back and level the man with a football-style tackle, but a pickup truck honked at him and swerved, and he continued on to the motel parking lot and got into his car.

He fumbled in his glove compartment for a few seconds, extracted a ballpoint pen, and dug his wallet out of his pocket. Inside, folded, was the napkin Zolene had given him with her aunt's address, the first day they had met. He scribbled Zolene's name and the address on the envelope, affixed two stamps there, and then inserted the old letter, wrapped in one of the copies. He hesitated, then wrote "I love you" on the copy, sealed the envelope, and drove out of the parking lot.

The white Lincoln was still there, and Bybee assumed that Sipes, after seeing the books, had surmised just what he was doing and had retreated into the bookstore to borrow the telephone, to call and to advise Lamar or LeGrand or Reed—or any other goon involved with them. Bybee drove slowly down Center Street, looking for only one thing, expecting at any second to see the sheriff's car behind him, or ahead, its lights flashing.

Near the church, he saw it: a mailbox. He pulled his car over, got out, and yanked the metal flap back and deposited the envelope with its old, creased letter inside. The envelope made a reassuring sound as it thumped into the bottom of the empty box, and Bybee returned to his car and drove quickly down the street. At 200 West, he turned left, then turned again, and headed straight up the street for the sheriff's office.

As he neared the place, he saw LeGrand pull away in the sheriff's car, pointed the other way and driving fast, unaware that Bybee was behind him. Bybee slowed, and when he saw that the car had turned at the next intersection, he parked at the curb. He opened his glove compartment again and pulled out any papers he found there: the order from Mackleprang appointing him to the case, his letter attached to it, some repair receipts, several sheets of notebook paper. After folding them into a dirty packet, he stuffed them into his rear hip pocket and got out of the car.

He walked up the sidewalk, his two books under his arm like a schoolboy on his way to class, opened the front door of the office, and went inside.

As it had done the day before, the police radio buzzed, crackling with static, and somewhere in the recesses of that dank office, another radio was on, this one tinkling out faint music. Marla Hamblin was at her desk, typing at a computer, the keyboard nearly smothered under her big, heavy bosom. Bybee walked over to her and smiled as she looked up.

"I need to see Lamar," he said. "The sheriff."

Marla shook her head. "I'm sorry, Sheriff Little's over to Hurricane."

Bybee waved one hand; the other gripped his books tight, trembling, and he took a deep breath to calm himself.

"Don't give me that, Marla." He pointed at a door that had a brass sign reading L. LITTLE tacked to it. "I know he's in there. Tell him Brig Bybee is here to talk about making arrangements to send Owen Parks home—everyone home."

The woman's sad eyes stayed on Bybee's own for a moment before she got up and walked over to the sheriff's door, opened it without knocking, and closed it behind her.

While he waited, Bybee stared at the wall behind Marla's desk, where a single, framed portrait hung. It was the most popular of all the poses, he guessed, the official one of the man—clear-eyed and solemn, his dark beard trimmed, his hair neat. It was the one seen in almost every church and ward hall in the state, one that, had Utah ever become the Republic of Deseret, would have hung in every government office, not just a few isolated holes like this.

He looked down at the book in his hand, at the shiny cover

and the photograph of the same man taken years later, after he had become bloated and white-haired, sated, regally carried about in a chair whenever he traveled.

The door to the private office opened, and Lamar Little came out with Marla in tow. He was not in uniform; instead he wore loose black pants and a white shirt that tented out from him like a tarp, his belly bulging against it.

"What do you want, Bybee?" the sheriff said. His breath was labored, a deep wheezing, and he smelled of sweat and, Bybee thought, cigarette smoke. Marla sat back at her desk and resumed her typing.

Bybee opened the Bible, extracted a copy of the letter, and pointed at the man's office. "In there," he said.

"You giving orders around har now, Bybee?"

"Yeah, I am, as a matter of fact," Bybee said. He pointed again at Lamar's office. "In there."

Lamar stood firm, unmoving, his labored breathing making his shoulders rise and fall, and then he mumbled something and turned around, indicating that Bybee should follow. They went into the office, and Lamar shut the door behind him.

The room was a miniature reproduction of the outer office: old oaken desks and chairs, metal file cabinets—and the smell of dirt and flatulence, and stale food, smoke. The one window, darkened with venetian blinds, let in little light, and the place was dark and oppressive.

"You have it?" Lamar said.

"Yes," Bybee said. He handed him the copy of the letter. "I guess this is what you wanted. Read it . . . and then we talk."

Lamar took the paper in his big, fleshy hands, and stopped. "This har is a copy."

"You bet it is," Bybee said. "Read it."

The sheriff pulled out a pair of glasses from his shirt pocket, fitted them over his big face, and began reading. As he did, Bybee took another copy and silently reviewed the letter that he had read twice at Zolene's Indian Cave, and twice again on his drive in from the ranch.

At the top, right-hand corner, it stated:

President's Office
Great Salt Lake City
Sept. 10, 1857

It was addressed to a man named Elder Isaac C. Haight, and the letter, in broad, swooping pen strokes, set forth the problems with federal troops advancing on the Utah territory, the soldiers' difficulties with rail supplies and livestock, and how God, once again, had smiled down upon the Mormons. Then, at the end, affixed almost as an afterthought, it read:

> *In regard to the Arkansas emigrants passing through your settlements, they must be immediately put out of the way. None, save those too young to talk, should be spared. You shall use your Indians as you please. Remember, they are the battle-axe of our Lord, and should be so employed.*
>
> *All is well with us. May the Lord bless you and all the Saints forever.*
>
> *Your Brother in the gospel of Christ.*
>
> *Brigham Young*

When Lamar had finished reading, he looked up, his massive face working. The office was silent except for the man's labored breathing, and he sat down in his chair, making it groan and creak, as though it might break.

Bybee stood in front of the desk. From outside the door the police radios' static welled, buzzing, and died, and outside, down the street, a child shouted.

"Well, there it is," Bybee said. "What everyone's been looking for. Is it just what you thought it would be, Lamar? Your prophet—our prophet—ordering the massacre of over a hundred people, most of them women and children."

"Shut your mouth!" Lamar said.

"Pretty tough when you actually see it, isn't it, Lamar? He *ordered* it, and you know the rest: he lied about it, and then stood by while someone was convicted in a kangaroo court and executed for it."

The sheriff said nothing, but his breathing was louder, as if he had been running—from something.

"It's hard to take, isn't it, Lamar, when you see the hard evidence? I felt the same when I first read it."

Lamar placed his forearms on his desk and leaned forward, his head drooping, the thick beard brushing the desktop. "It's . . . a copy."

Bybee held up the book he had just purchased—a coffee-table biography of Brigham Young—and tossed it on the desk in front of the sheriff's face, where it landed with a loud *thwack*, the photograph of the great Mormon Moses glaring up at him.

"Here," Bybee said. "In the middle of that book. Compare the signatures in there to the one on this letter. Yeah, it's a copy, but a copy of the real McCoy, of Brigham Young ordering the slaughter."

Lamar hawked up a gob of phlegm, and for an instant, Bybee thought he was going to spit it at him, but he swallowed it and cleared his throat.

"You're playing pretty dangerous games, Bybee. We had a deal."

Bybee straightened and took another long, slow breath. "Yeah, I know. And *you* know I didn't kill Watters, and that Parks didn't kill Farnsworth—but you probably know who did, or who's really responsible. So, here's the deal, the real deal: you release Parks. You justify it any way you want, do it any way you want, work it out with Hightower, but just release him, let him go home. And you forget about arresting and prosecuting me, too. Then you drag whoever *did* commit those murders out into the daylight. And you can do that however you want. But just do it."

"You're crazy," Lamar said.

"Maybe so," Bybee said. He pointed at the letter in the sheriff's hands. "But you do all that, then the original of that letter is destroyed."

Lamar lifted his head and stared at Bybee, his eyes hooded,

almost closed, almost lost in the thick folds of pale flesh. Behind him, on a wooden hat rack, hung his gray uniform shirt and his holstered pistol and gun belt, and he swiveled in his chair and looked at it.

Bybee's heart was thumping crazily in his chest. "Too late for that," he said. "I've got the original locked up. I end up dead in that lake tonight, or with a hole in my head in a basement, this thing goes to someone who knows what to do with it, who to give it to. And it won't be Sipes or the church."

Lamar cleared his throat again. "How do I know you jes' won't keep it, anyway?"

Bybee laughed. "You got to have faith, Sheriff. I'm an honorable man, like you. Remember?"

Lamar leaned back, out of the weak light, and into the shadows. "And if I don't do what you want?"

"Then I go to trial tomorrow," Bybee said, "as planned." He pulled out the folded pack of meaningless papers from his hip pocket and held them up. "Watters gave me these the night he was killed. They're his notes, a trial script, they lay out everything I need to know to make sure Parks walks."

Lamar stared at the wad of papers in Bybee's hands as if they were holy scripture, a message from beyond the grave.

"And at trial," Bybee went on, "I shoot the state's case all to hell. Then, when it's my turn"—he pointed again at Lamar's copy of the letter—"I introduce the original of that into evidence. The prosecutor can object, can fight it; can raise all kinds of hell, and Reed can scream and yell and hold me in contempt. But one way or another, whether it's for witness impeachment, for the appeal, for . . . whatever, I'll get it into the record. And once I do, you asshole, it's *public* record, and every goddamned anti-Mormon reporter in this state with an ax to grind will have a copy by the next day. And Parks probably walks, to boot."

"You're crazy," Lamar said. His face was wet with sweat now, and he ran his fat hand across his forehead. "You tried the same bullshit against Bellard, against the church."

"You're right. But this time, it's going to stick." He pointed at the biography on the desk. "I'm going to use that; I'm going to bring a handwriting expert down from Beaver—" He was lying now, even more, fabricating and inventing as he went along, his eyes dancing now, alive. He knew Watters had blurted out something about an expert at the Buckskin, but he wasn't sure who or what kind. "He'll testify that the letter is the real McCoy," Bybee said, "and everyone will finally know what the church has been covering up all these years. The same way they've been covering for Sipes. God knows who else."

Lamar's bulk seemed to shift, to sift downward, sinking. "Why are you doing this, Bybee? Reed says you've always been stuck in low gear. Didn't care much."

"Well, I'm in high now."

"But you're LDS—or war."

"I was part-time, Lamar. But I'll tell you; I've always been looking for a reason to really join this church, not half-ass it; looking for something that will convince me that things are not twisted and screwed up like Sipes has twisted them or"—he nodded at the letter under the sheriff's hands—"like others have. A few nights ago, I found that reason. Zolene Swapp and I sat at the Gazebo over here and watched everyone dance and have a good time. And I realized that those people are happy and content because they believe in something good. It's that simple. But they have been *told* these things are real and good. It's not what they know."

"Thar's no reason to know."

"Maybe not. But if I turn that letter loose, people *are* going to know, and some are going to end up like me, always questioning the church and what they've been taught and told. Oh, it won't destroy the church, like all the rumors said; it won't come crashing down, but it will make a lot of those people at the park start to doubt things, and might have them calling this religion the one nasty word it's been fighting since it all began."

"What's that?" Lamar said.

Bybee moved several inches closer, inclining his lanky body toward the man, almost whispering. "A cult."

Lamar folded his hands on his desk and said nothing. Bybee straightened and studied him, searched him, wondering if the sheriff, as a young man, had ever been on a mission—somewhere, anywhere—and gone "tracting," as they called it, bicycling or tramping from door to door or hut to hut with the *Book of Mormon* in his backpack, hawking this new, blond-haired brand of salvation, a wholly American style of redemption, the Third Coming, Christ promising to appear in the New World again . . . but this time in Missouri.

Lamar suddenly stood up and walked heavily to his door and opened it.

"Good-bye, Bybee," he said. "Thanks for the Sunday school lesson."

15

BEFORE Euzell Brimhall became the bailiff and groundskeeper at the courthouse, he had owned the Moqui Riding Stables, just east of town and not far from Hell's Bellows. He rarely sold his horses, keeping them their entire, plodding lives until they finally began to balk at carrying any more fat tourists, to stumble and collapse.

When that happened, Euzell—a wiry, gray-haired cowboy—would spend an entire day carefully grooming the animal, even trimming its mane and digging muck out of its hooves, all the while talking to the dying animal, murmuring, stroking it.

Then, satisfied, he would lead the poor creature down a narrow path to a shallow wash behind the stables and, giving the horse a last pat on its neck, step back and fire a bullet through its brain.

Now he had prepared the Kane County Courthouse for today's trial in the same way, for the same reason. He had carefully mowed the small patch of grass in front, trimmed the shrubbery, edged the walkway with hand clippers, and even swept the small parking lot in the rear.

Finished, his tools and the dead grass and leaves heaped in the back of his truck, he stepped back and surveyed his work, the orange crane and its wrecking ball swaying, just behind it all, waiting.

Bybee sat on the oaken pew outside the judge's office, his forearms resting on his thighs, and hung his head in front of him as though he were sick. He was dressed in his best suit, a silver-flecked red tie, and polished shoes, his black hair oiled and combed neatly in place. But he looked worn, drained by a night of half-sleep and strange dreams.

At the other end of the dim hall, the double doors to the courtroom had been opened, and in the middle of the room, toward the front, he could see Owen Parks sitting at one of the wooden counsel tables, the oversize sport coat draped on him, the bow tie crooked and comical. Behind him, dressed in his starched, gray uniform, stood LeGrand Little, his hands hooked to his belt.

There was a thumping on the wooden stairs, a jumbled, clumsy sound, as though a cow or a horse were struggling to the second floor. After a moment, DeWitt Hightower appeared, followed by Brimhall, the bailiff, and they tramped down the hall, in step now—a sad, hollow cadence, like an honor guard —and came pounding up to Bybee. Brimhall nodded and, withdrawing a tangle of keys, opened the judge's door and retreated, and Hightower motioned for Bybee to follow him inside the office.

Hightower closed the door and faced Bybee. He was dressed in the same wrinkled beige suit he wore the first day they had met, in this very office, but instead of his big leather briefcase, he carried only a manila envelope tucked under his arm. Behind him, framed by the window behind the judge's desk, the orange crane was poised, and the bright morning sun glinted off it.

"I'm sorry about Watters," Hightower said. His fat lips looked rubbery and wet, greasy, and he puffed out his cheeks and exhaled. "It was a terrible thing."

"It was," Bybee said. He waited, watching Hightower's face, looking down at him, looking for any hint that the man knew what truly happened to Watters, any hint that he was in league with Lamar and the others.

"Should be a lesson to everyone," Hightower said. "Drinking, getting drunk . . . going swimming. . . ."

"Yeah," Bybee said. He felt himself relax, something disengaging inside of him, a palpable twitch. Dewitt was a good man, after all. "It's a shame."

Hightower nodded, agreeing, but he already seemed disinterested, focused on something else, and he sat down in a wooden chair and motioned for Bybee to do the same. The prosecutor puffed out his cheeks again and stared at the crane, then opened his folder and looked at Bybee. His small eyes were tired, raw, and Bybee wondered if the man had spent the same sort of evening he had—tossing, pacing, knotted up with it all.

"I had a crappy night," Hightower said. He looked sad, defeated. "Got a visit from Lamar Little, the sheriff, along with an Indian named Jerome . . . something. Called himself Old Jay."

"Old Jay," Bybee repeated. It was one of the last things Watters had mentioned to him. "Lives at the Red Land Roost."

"Yeah," Hightower said. He tried to smile and then shook his head. "Cripes, I guess you were way ahead of me on this one. I should have figured Brig Bybee had something up his sleeve."

Bybee shrugged, his straight shoulders almost bouncing. "Well, we were working the case, DeWitt. What did Old Jay tell you?"

"Oh, c'mon, Bybee. What you and Watters knew all along. Parks's camper was in the south end of that trailer park—across the state line. It was sitting in Arizona, for God's sake."

Bybee squinted, trying to camouflage his shock. "Bad search."

"Damned right, 'bad search.' Utah cops executing a Utah search warrant in Arizona. Judge Mackleprang would have personally flushed that Polaroid down a toilet and read me the riot act."

"Maybe."

"You guys were setting me up."

Bybee smiled confidently, remembering that Watters had mentioned a map, and realizing that was what his expert was for: to testify about the precise jurisdictional location of Parks's camper. But he was still perplexed. "What else?"

"Oh, the Indian, the old guy, told me that Parks had been drinking beer with him in the afternoon—Thanksgiving—same time Farnsworth was killed. The other Indians were there, too; they lied in their statements. He could prove that." He shook his head, embarrassed. "Cripes, I would have been standing there . . . " He stopped and held his hands out, helpless.

Bybee began to finish the old line—*with your dick hanging out*—but this was a good, solid, tithe-paying Mormon man sitting in front of him. "Flat-footed?" he said.

"Yeah. Flat-footed. Worse. Anyway, I guess I really admire Sheriff Little for having the guts to come forward."

"Lamar's a good man," Bybee said.

"He is," Hightower said. His eyes suddenly focused on the far wall, at something distant, sublime—pure. "He is, at that."

"So what's going to happen, DeWitt?"

Hightower opened the manila folder he had in his lap and took out several pieces of paper. "I drew these up last night and went over to Judge Mackleprang's room. I wasn't trying to ex parte you, but I figured you wouldn't mind."

Bybee felt his heart racing, the heat spreading from his scalp downward. "What is it?"

"It's a motion to dismiss the case—along with the order of dismissal signed by the judge. Jeopardy hasn't attached, so if it turns out I'm wrong, if we get other evidence on Parks, I can always grab him again."

"So you're dismissing."

"I am. Trial's off. Your client can go home."

Bybee felt the same way he had the first day he had sat here, in the same chair: wobbly, out of balance.

"Thank you, DeWitt."

"Well," Hightower said, "I can't go to trial with this evidence. Shoot, I have no evidence."

Bybee leaned forward, extended his hand, and gripped Hightower's thick palm, firmly, for several seconds.

"Thank you," Bybee said again. "This is right. Parks is as innocent as they come."

"Oh, cripes, Bybee. I've been doing this stuff as long as you have. They all say they're innocent."

"Believe me," Bybee said, "in this case, he is."

"Well . . ." Hightower trailed off and looked at his watch. "I guess we need the judge here, a court reporter. I need to get a few things on the record."

"Sure."

The two men fell silent, and an awkwardness settled over the room as they waited for Mackleprang. Bybee walked behind the desk and looked out through the tall window. He could see a sizable section of the town, the wide, shady streets that pushed up under the cliffs, the big white *K* that presided over everything.

Bybee knew that Lamar and his men—the Daughter of Zion, for lack of a better or more conventional term—had fulfilled half of the bargain. The second part, the more difficult and demanding part, was probably not ever going to occur, but it would not matter. On a grander order, in the "cosmic scheme of things," as people liked to say, retribution for two deaths in the middle of nowhere was insignificant, paltry. Thousands around the globe and throughout history were regularly and systematically slaughtered, but when they were, the earth never wobbled, the sun did not spark or flare for a second or two, the heavens did not split open. . . .

Bybee turned away from the window, and while Hightower sat, tired and deflated, in his chair, he poked around the office. The map of Utah, he saw, was nearly an antique, the framed pictures on the wall were of judges who were either dead or retired, and the case reporters in the sagging shelves were hopelessly out of date, useless. He withdrew one of the volumes, and when he did, he saw, behind it on the shelf, something plastic, an instrument of some sort with a clear, plastic window and a rubber eyepiece . . . a camera, a Polaroid camera . . .

"Lord . . ."

Somewhere in the darkened bowels of the courthouse, a woman screamed, a shrill, anguished sound that echoed down the hall. Hightower sat bolt upright in his chair, and Bybee hurried to the door and threw it open.

The woman screamed again; it came from the first floor, and Bybee ran down the hall, glimpsing Parks in the courtroom for a second, sitting bug-eyed, while LeGrand hovered by him, confused, unsure what to do.

He clattered down the stairs, just behind Brimhall, and ran into the darkened ground floor. Donell Bunting, the cook at the Pow-Wow Wild West tourist show, stood just inside the main door, sobbing, her stained apron still wrapped around her.

Brimhall came up to her and took her by the arm, and the woman half collapsed and fell against him.

"The town," she said. She pointed south, toward Center Street, then began shrieking again so loudly that Brimhall clasped his hand over her mouth and eased her over to a wooden pew.

"The town," she said again.

Bybee knew what she meant, and he pushed open the door. A few people who had probably trailed after the woman, alarmed, stood in the front, and he hurried past them.

He sprinted down the sidewalk, and at Center Street he crossed the intersection, dodging cars and RVs, and burst into the Pow-Wow. A woman was huddled in the corner, crying, and Dell Glazier, the owner, in his black shirt and big black Stetson, was desperately punching the buttons on a telephone, cursing.

Bybee ran through the store, past the tourist junk and the lunch counter in the rear, pushed open the rear door, and emerged into the phony frontier town.

In the middle of the dirt street, at the gallows, a man hung from a rope by his neck, his face dark, his blackened tongue partly out of his mouth. A crude square had been cut in the plank floor of the gallows, and the sawed-off pieces of lumber lay on the ground around it.

There were several other people nearby, part of the Pow-Wow kitchen crew, a tourist or two, and Bybee walked past them toward the gallows. The latrine stench of raw feces immediately stung him, and he covered his nose and mouth with his hand and walked closer to the man who dangled there.

It was Sipes. He was in his suit—the same one Bybee had seen him in the day before—but his shirt was torn, the tie gone, and his pants were wet with excrement and urine. His face—his entire head—looked smaller, somehow, and his eyes were half open, as though he were squinting, trying to see more clearly, to fathom it all.

Someone put a hand on his shoulder, and Bybee turned around and looked into Lamar Little's big, bloated face.

"Damn shame," the sheriff said. His voice was deeper than normal, husky. He put his mouth close to Bybee's ear, his breath hot and foul. "We have a deal. Best keep it."

Bybee looked over the sheriff's shoulder at a group of people that had gathered there, some of the women crying, turning away. In the rear he saw Reed Mackleprang, his round, pale head hovering like a balloon above the others, and when their eyes met, the judge turned and disappeared. In his place, the two young Indians, Fall and Burton, appeared, staring solemnly at the hanging man, their faces like polished mahogany.

The sheriff saw Bybee staring at the Indians. "Those boys do pretty good wark, don't they?" he said.

Bybee pointed at the hanging man. "You killed him."

"He killed himself."

"Lord God."

Lamar turned away from Bybee. "All right," he yelled, pointing at several men close by. "Let's cut this guy down."

Dell Glazier and two other men stepped forward and walked slowly toward the gallows.

"Anyone know who he is?" Lamar said. "War he's from?"

16

In Kanab, there have never been street decorations at Christmas, no Easter parades, not even flags and fireworks on Independence Day, a few weeks earlier. But on July 24 this lidded, simmering reserve suddenly boils over and bubbles down the streets in a parade that celebrates the state's queer history of bearded pioneers and buckboard Saints.

And the parade this year in Kanab was the same as always: a squeaking, tooting blare of the high school marching band, followed by a train of horse-drawn buckboards and miniature Conestogas, and after that, a ragtag collection of cars and trucks and bicycles, all in a tangle of crepe paper. Women, old and young alike, in long dresses and bonnets, rode atop the wagons, while the men, their beards full and proud now, tramped alongside with their sons in tow, all waving rifles and six-shooters in the air.

The most glorious day of the year had descended upon Deseret. The sun was out, the sky was clear, and the air virtually hummed with tradition and vibrated with history. Hundreds of townsfolk and tourists lined Center Street; children perched atop shoulders; cameras clicked; dogs yapped and people laughed; and at the Gazebo, row after row of tables sagged under the weight of the grand feast that a dozen good female Saints were laying out.

It was *the* day, the *only* day—it was Pioneer Day—the day Brigham Young had reestablished the kingdom of Zion, the New Jerusalem. It was his day; it was Brigham's day.

"This is the right place!" someone yelled. It was Dell Glazier standing in the lead wagon, dressed in fringed buckskin and a cowboy hat, one hand resting on his swollen belly, the other waving a rifle in the air.

"This is the right place!" he yelled again.

But from a crowd of sandaled and sunglassed American tourists standing in front of Duke's, a man stepped out into the street.

"For what?" he yelled back, and his friends laughed.

Bybee sat on the Pow-Wow porch on a bench next to the wooden Indian and watched the parade crawl by. The store was one of the few that was open on this state holiday, and tourists milled on the porch and inside, most still puzzled by the midsummer parade. There were still some reporters around, mostly from Salt Lake, taking endless pictures of the town—the real town and the Pow-Wow's make-believe town—following up on the story that had dominated the news in Utah, and around the country, for the past three days: the death of Bellard Sipes, the anointed one, the heir apparent, and his suicide note, found later, which confessed to two murders.

The tail end of the procession finally crawled by, and a squad of young boys in phony cotton beards fanned out across the street with shovels and plastic bags and scooped up the wet, greenish droppings of the animals. The tourists applauded and cheered—this they understood.

"Brig!"

Bybee turned and saw Zolene limping down the sidewalk, weaving in and out of the revelers, who by now, at parade's end, had broken ranks and were spreading out. She waved, and he waved back, and in a moment she was on the Pow-Wow porch and making her way toward him. She was in jeans and her "U of A" T-shirt, and she carried the same purse she had the night of the Gazebo dance.

He stood up, and they embraced, tightly. Bybee drew back but kept one hand on her hip.

"I was hoping I would see you," he said.

Zolene smiled; she looked rested, her eyes clear. "Well, now you see me."

Bybee motioned toward the bench, and the two of them sat down, their hips and legs touching, and watched the latter-day pioneers—the remnants of the parade—stream back down Center Street in the opposite direction, heading for the Gazebo and the food there.

"I guess you're leaving," Bybee said.

Zolene nodded. "Yes. I have to. My kids probably don't even remember what I look like."

Bybee turned and openly appraised her, the breathless beauty of her, and shook his head. "That's pretty hard to do."

She smiled, embarrassed, and they watched a teenage girl across the street struggle out of her long-sleeved blouse and dark hoop skirt and emerge, like a butterfly, in pink shorts and a T-shirt. Behind her a fat boy with a toy six-gun came up, spun her around, and pretended to accost her, gently poking the barrel in her stomach, a pantomime of violence that everyone in town knew now was all too real here, of late.

"Brig," Zolene said, "I'm not sure what you did, what has happened, but—" She stopped, aware that the nightmare had culminated just behind her, in the frontier town, where she had once stood and grinned and mugged for the camera.

"Well, it's over," Bybee said.

"But what happens to the others? Lamar and LeGrand . . . whoever else?"

"Nothing," he said. "LeGrand probably gets elected sheriff, Lamar retires and goes fishing, Mackleprang keeps driving around Utah trying cases." He shrugged and watched the play pioneers troop by, laughing, teasing one another. "Life just goes on as usual."

"And you?" Zolene said. "You go on 'as usual'?"

"Yeah, I guess. I'm going back to Beaver, but I don't know what I'll do. I swore that this was my last case. Maybe it is."

Zolene took his hand and gently held it, stroking his knuckles. "Am I going to see you again?"

Bybee looked at her and squeezed her hand, hard. "Yes, Zolene, you will."

"Good." She smiled. "What are you doing for Thanksgiving?"

"I don't know. It's a ways off. I'll probably spend it with Brileena, my daughter—maybe even say hello to Helena—but . . . I don't know."

"Well, why don't you come down to Tucson the next day, the day after? I'm in the book. We can have dinner . . . another dinner. Things will have cooled down by then. . . ."

Bybee understood the double meaning, and he slipped his arm around her waist and brought her close to him. "I can wait. I'll be there."

"Good."

They sat silently for several moments until Zolene bent down and picked up her purse from the porch. She opened it and pulled out the envelope Bybee had mailed her three days before. She took out the yellowed letter, still intact from its brief trip through the mails, and held it out to him.

"You can have this," she said.

Bybee shook his head. "Why would I want it?"

Zolene bent her head back and pulled her hair out of her face. "Because I know you used it, somehow. You used it to finally get to the truth—at least part of it. I suppose that makes it yours."

"No, it doesn't."

She held out the letter. "Take it, anyway. I don't want it."

Bybee slowly reached out, took the letter, and held it in his hand, feeling again the parchmentlike texture, the thin fragility of it, its tactile horror. He suddenly got to his feet and walked into the Pow-Wow, and a moment later, came back out holding a plastic lighter he had just bought. He peeled away the cellophane wrapper and held the lighter and the letter in his hands.

"Are you sure, Brig?" Zolene said. "Someone might pay a lot of money for that."

In front of them, a couple in frontier garb walked by them, whispering, and in the middle of the street the man stopped and lifted his hat and kissed the woman on the mouth, and she laughed and took off her bonnet. She shook her long hair free, and the two of them, arm in arm, walked toward the park and the other Saints gathering there.

"I'm sure," Bybee said.

He took the lighter in one hand, flicked it on, and held it to the edge of the letter. A tiny finger of flame crept up one side, and in seconds the whole thing was afire, the old, dried paper combusting like a handful of straw. Bybee dropped it on the porch, and while a few tourists looked on, confused, the two of them watched it burn out. Finally he ground the ashes of the letter into the wood slats until there was nothing left but a gray, dirty smear.

"I guess that's that," Zolene said. She stood up. "I've got to get going. Don't want to drive in the dark."

Bybee walked with her off the porch and up the sidewalk until they reached her Mustang parked on a side street. From there they could easily see the back half of the courthouse, already in ruins, half standing amid the rubble, as though hit by a bomb. He opened the door for her and held it while she got in the car and fished through her purse for her keys. She found them and then looked up at Bybee through the window.

"I mean it, Brig. The day after Thanksgiving. I'll be waiting."

"I'll be there," he said.

Dell Glazier, still in his buckskin outfit, was now riding a spotted horse down Center Street, waving a big cowboy hat at everyone he saw, including the two of them, and Bybee waved back.

Zolene started the car and, from atop her visor, unclipped a pair of sunglasses and slipped them on. She dropped the car into gear and checked her mirror, but before she pulled away, she looked up at Bybee. She mouthed something, several words, silently, and Bybee could only guess—only hope—what they were.

She drove slowly away, turning onto Center Street, and weaved carefully through the modern pioneers until she disappeared at the curve at the end of town.

Bybee walked back to the Pow-Wow, stared briefly at the smear of ashes on the porch, and moved on. He had walked here from his tepee, enjoying the day, knowing the same kind of parade was going on in Beaver, everywhere, the way it had when he was a child, the way it had, and would, forever.

He walked by the Book Outpost and stopped. There, in the display window, were dozens of books, all propped up to show the pictures of the old Mormon prophets and pioneers who had built and rebuilt the church, who had, out of a mist, fashioned something real.

There was Joseph Smith, of course, and Brigham Young, and all the others: John Taylor, and Oliver Cowdery and Rigdon, and the frontier heroes—Snow, Hamblin, Pratt—even John D. Lee, blurred, his eyes lost beneath the thick eyebrows as he gazed calmly at his executioners.

And at one end were the more recent champions of the church, men in business suits who had fortified the empire and then sealed the past.

Bybee looked at the book jackets and at the faces that seemed to stare directly back at him, questioning him. They were faces of men who all knew the secrets, knew the truth, and he could hear them now, a gruff murmur from behind the glass, a rustling from another life.

He looked up from the books, and in the window he saw that, behind the display, there was another sheet of glass, and he saw two faint reflections of himself, one within the other, as though his body had become a transparent shell and he could see, within it, his own soul.

He walked to the glassed door, but the clerk, the thin, unhappy-looking woman, stood inside and shook her head. She said one word—a word airy and distant behind the glass, a word that arose from a century and a half away, a word that had seeped up through the layers of years, of lies.

"Closed," she said.

Epilogue

MOUNTAIN MEADOWS, UTAH
MARCH 23, 1877, 10:20 A.M.

The man in the gray coat nods and walks back to the knot of men at the wagon. John removes his hat and muffler and then wriggles from his coat and hands it to another man who has come up beside him. He sits back down upon the box and turns his face toward the five men who have hastily assembled before him, not twenty feet away, but whom he cannot see because of the binding just placed over his eyes.

—Center the heart, boys. Don't mangle my body.

There is a pause while the five ready themselves, and then another signal is given and five shots are fired and John D. Lee tumbles backward into his open coffin, where he lies, his heart ripped by bullets. Both legs hang ludicrously over the sides of the coffin, and one arm remains upraised, wedged against the wood and his cold face, as if in a salute.

Two men quickly straighten the body in the coffin, nail the cover firmly upon it, and with the help of two others, load it upon the wagon. After most of the men disperse, the wagon owner climbs atop the plank seat and drives the coffin out of Mountain Meadows and back toward Parowan, to a family that awaits it there.